ASSIGNMENT IN NOWHERE

KEITH LAUMER
is also the author of
- WORLDS OF THE IMPERIUM
- GALACTIC ODYSSEY
- IT'S A MAD MAD MAD GALAXY
- THE MONITORS
- THE OTHER SIDE OF TIME
- THE OTHER SKY
- CATASTROPHE PLANET

ASSIGNMENT IN NOWHERE

KEITH LAUMER

LONDON
DENNIS DOBSON

Copyright © 1968 by Keith Laumer

All rights reserved

First published in Great Britain in 1972
Dobson Books Ltd., 80 Kensington Church Street, London W8
Printed by Latimer Trend & Co. Ltd., Whitstable, Kent.
ISBN 0 234 77632 3

PROLOGUE

He sat astride the great war-horse, in the early morning, looking across the field toward the mist-obscured heights where the enemy waited. The chain-mail coif and hauberk weighed heavy on him; and there was another weight within him: a sense of a thing undone, a duty forgotten, of something valuable betrayed.

"The mist clears, my lord," Trumpington spoke at his side. "Will you attack?"

He looked up at the sun, burning through the mist. He thought of the green vales of home, and the sense grew in him that death waited here on this obscure field.

"No. I'll not unsheathe Balingore this day," he said at last.

"My lord—is all well with you?" There was concern in the young squire's voice.

He nodded curtly. Then he turned and rode back through the silent, staring ranks of his panoplied host.

Chapter One

At Molly's place, the jukebox was breaking its heart over a faithless woman, but there was nobody listening but a few conchs sitting out on the rickety porch under the yellow bug lights, nursing beers and catching the breeze moving in off the gulf. It was after nine P.M. and the heat of the day was gone from the beach, and the surf coming up on the sand sounded lonesome and far away, like an old man's memories.

I took a stool at the bar and Molly put a bottle of wine in front of me, with the seal still intact.

"Johnny, it happened again today," she said. "I found a platter I swear I broke last month, right there in the sink, not a chip out of it. And the whiskey stock is different—stuff I never ordered there, and not a sign of the Red Label—and you know I know my stock. And three heads of cabbage, fresh yesterday—rotten in the cooler!"

"So—your last order was mixed up—and the vegetables weren't as fresh as they looked," I said.

"And toadstools growing in the corners?" she said. "I guess that's natural too? You know better'n that, John Curlon! And how about this?" She brought a heavy cut-glass cup up from behind the bar. It was about one-quart capacity, rounded on the bottom, with a short stem.

"This was here when I came in this evening. It's worth money. How'd it get here?"

"Impulse shopping," I suggested.

"Don't kid me, Johnny. There's something happening—something that scares me! It's like the world was shifting right under my feet! And its not just here! I see things all round—little things—like trees are in different places than they used to be—and a magazine I started reading; when I came back to it—there wasn't any such story in the book!"

I patted her hand and she caught my fingers. "Johnny—tell me what's happening—what to do! I'm not losing my mind, am I?"

"You're fine, Molly. The glass was probably the gift of some secret admirer. And everybody loses things sometimes, or remembers things a little differently than they really were. You'll probably find your story in another magazine. You just got mixed up." I tried to make it sound convincing, but it's hard to do when you're not sure yourself.

"And Johnny—what about you?" Molly was still holding my hand. "Have you talked to *them* yet?"

"Who?" I asked.

She gave me a hot look from a pair of eyes that had probably been heartbreakers back before the Key West sun had bleached the fire out of them. "Don't act like you don't know what I mean! There was another one in today asking for you—a new guy, one I never saw before."

"Oh—them. No, I haven't had time—"

"Johnny! Smarten up! You can't buck that crowd. They'll smash you so flat you could slide under the linoleum without making a bump."

"Don't worry about me, Molly—"

"Sure, grin! Johnny Curlon, six foot three of bone and muscle, the fellow with the bullet-proof hide! Listen, Johnny! That Jakesy's a mean one—especially since they put the wire in his jaw. He'll chop you into cut-bait—" she broke off. "But I guess you know all that. I guess nothing I can say is going to change you." She turned and picked a Rémy Martin bottle from the back bar.

"Like you said, it's just a glass. Might as well use it." She poured brandy into the chalice and I picked it up and looked into the glint of amber light inside it. The glass was cool and smooth and heavy against my palms. . . .

Seated in my great chair, I looked down at the narrow, treacherous face of him I had loved so well, saw hope leap up in those crafty eyes.

"My lord king," he started, and shuffled toward me on his knees, dragging the chains that he bore. "I know not why I was cajoled to embark on such rude folly. 'Twas but a fit of madness, meaning naught—"

"Three times ere now have you sought my throne and crown," I cried, not for his ears alone, but for all those who might murmur against that which I knew must be. "Three times have I pardoned thee, lavished anew my favor on thee, raised thee up before loyal men."

"Heaven's grace descend on thy Majesty for thy great mercy," the glib voice babbled, and even in that moment I saw the hunger in his eyes. "This time, I swear—"

"Swear not, thou who art forsworn!" I commanded him. "Rather think on thy soul, to tarnish it no more in these thy final hours!"

And I saw fear dawn at last, driving out the hunger and all else save lust for life itself. And I knew that lust to be foredoomed.

"Mercy, brother," he gasped, and raised his manacled hands to me as to a god. "Mercy, out of memory of past joys shared! Mercy, for love of our mother, the sainted Lady Eleanor—"

"Foul not the name of her who loved thee!" I shouted, hardening my heart against the vision of her face, pale under the hand of approaching death, swearing me to the eternal protection of him who knelt before me.

He wept as they bore him away, wept and swore his true allegiance and love for me. And later in my chambers, drugged with wine, I wept, hearing again and ever again the fall of the headsman's ax.

They told me that at the end, he found his manhood, and walked to the block with his head held high, as befits the son of kings. And with his last words, he forgave me.

Oh, he forgave me. . . .

A voice was calling my name. I blinked and saw Molly's face as through a haze of distance.

"Johnny—what is it?"

I shook my head and the hallucination faded. "I don't know," I said. "Not getting enough sleep, maybe."

"Your face," she said. "When you took the glass in your hands and held it up like that, you looked—like a stranger . . ."

"Maybe it reminded me of something."

"It's getting to you too, isn't it, Johnny?"

"Maybe." I drank the brandy off in a gulp.

"The best thing for you would be to go away," she said softly. "You know that."

"There doesn't have to be any trouble. All they have to do is stay out of my way."

"And if they don't?"

"You can't have everything," I said.

She looked at me and sighed.

"I guess I knew all along you'd go your own way, Johnny," she said.

I felt her eyes following me as I pushed through the screen door and out into the cool evening air.

2

A heavy fog had rolled in from the gulf, and down at the pier the big merc lamps were shining through the mist like a bridge out into nowhere. At the end of it, my boat floated in fog. She was a sweet forty-footer, almost paid for, riding low in the water with full loads in her four hundred-gallon tanks. The pair of 480 Supermarine Chryslers under her hatches were old, but in top condition; I'd rebuilt them myself. They'd always gotten me where I was going, and back again.

I went up past the gear locker by the pole and two men separated themselves from the shadows and stepped out to block my way. One of them was the big ex-pug, the one they call Jakesy. The other was a foxy little bird in racetrack clothes. He flipped a cigarette away and pinched the knot in his tie and shook out his cuffs like a card shark getting set for a fast shuffle.

"This here is Mr. Renata, Curlon," Jakesy said. Somebody had hit him in the throat once and his voice was a foghorn whisper. "He came down from Palm special to talk to ya."

"A pleasure, Mr. Curlon," the foxy man put out a long narrow hand like a monkey's. I didn't look at it.

"I told you not to hang around my boat," I said.

"Don't get tough, Curlon," Jakesy said. "Mr. Renata's a big man, he come a long way—"

"The Fishermen's Protective Association's an important organization, fella," Renata spoke up. "A man can save hisself a lot of trouble by signing up."

"Why would I want to save myself trouble?"

He nodded, as if I'd said something reasonable. "Tell you what, Curlon," he said. "To show our good will, we'll waive the three hundred initiation fee."

"Just stay out of my way," I said, and started past him.

"Wait a minute, conch," Jakesy growled. "Mugs like you don't talk to Mr. Renata that way."

"Take it easy, Jakesy," Renata said softly. "Mr. Curlon's too smart a man to start any trouble."

I looked the way his eyes had flicked and saw the car that had eased up across the street. Two men had gotten out and were leaning against the front fender with their arms folded.

"You got to move with the times, Curlon," Renata said, and showed me some teeth that needed work. "A guy on his own ain't got a chance nowadays. The competition is too tough." He took some papers out of an inside pocket and held them out. "Sign 'em, fella. It's the smart thing to do."

I took the papers and tore them across the middle and

tossed them away. "Anything else before you go?" I asked him. His face got nasty, but he put out a hand to hold Jakesy back.

"That's too bad, Curlon. Too bad." He took out his show hanky and flapped it and I stepped in fast past him and left-hooked Jakesy before his hand had time to finish its sweep up from his hip. The blackjack went flying and Jakesy took two off-balance steps back and went over the side and hit with plenty of splash. I grabbed for Renata, and a small automatic fell out of his clothes; he dived for it and ran into the toe of my shoe. He flopped out on his back, spitting blood and mewling like a wet kitten. The two back-up men were coming at a run. I grabbed up the gun and started to say something to Renata about calling them off, but a gun flashed and coughed through a silencer and a slug cut air past my right ear. I fired twice from the hip and a man skidded and went down and the other hit the planks. I caught Renata's collar and hauled him to his feet.

"Any closer and you're dead," I said; he kicked and tried to bite my hand, then squalled an order.

"The lousy punk got Jimmy," the yell came back.

Renata yelled again and one of the gunnies got to his feet, slowly.

"Jimmy, too," I said. Renata passed the word. The man on his feet tried to lift his partner, couldn't make it, settled for getting a couple of handfuls of coat and dragging him. After a minute or two I heard the car start up, gun away into the fog.

"OK—now gimme a break," Renata said. I pushed him away. "Sure," I said, and hit him hard in the stomach, and when he bent over, I slammed a solid one to the chin. I left him on the dock and went on out and started up. I used my old knife to cut her stern line; in two minutes I was nosed out into the channel, headed for deep water. I watched the beach lights sliding away into the mist that covered the decay and the poverty and just left the magic of a harbor at night. And the smell of corruption; it couldn't cover that.

I ran due west for five hours, then switched off and sat on deck and watched the stars for an hour, listening for the sound of engines, but nobody was chasing me.

I put out a sea anchor and went below and turned in.

3

There was a low mist across the water when I rolled out just before dawn. My shoulder was aching, and for a minute that and the feel of the clammy fog against my face almost reminded me of something: the glint of light on steel and a pennon that fluttered in the breeze, and the feel of a big horse under me; and that was pretty strange, because I've never been on a horse in my life.

The boat was dead still on the flat sea, and even through the mist the sun already had some heat in it. It looked like another of those wide, blue days on the gulf, with the sea and sky empty to the far horizon. Out here, Jakesy and his boss Renata seemed like something out of another life. I started for the galley to rustle some ham and eggs, noticed a curious thing: little clumps of funguslike stuff, growing on the mahogany planking and on the chrome rail. I kicked it over the side and spent half an hour swabbing her down and polishing her brass, listening to a silence as big as the world. Afterward, I lifted the hatch and checked the engines over, screwed the grease cups on the stuffing boxes down a turn or two. When I came back up on deck, there was a man standing by the port rail, looking at me over the sights of a gun.

4

He was dressed in a tight white uniform with little twists of gold braid at the cuffs. His face was lean, hard, not sunburned; a city man. The thing in his hand wasn't like any gun I had ever seen, but it had that functional look; and the hand that pointed it at my face was as steady as it needed to be. I looked past him, all around the boat. There was no other boat in sight—not even a rubber raft.

"Smooth," I said. "How did you manage it?"

"This is a neurac—a nerve-gun," he said in a matter-of-fact tone. "It is indescribably painful. Do exactly as I tell you and I won't be forced to use it." He motioned me back toward the hatch. He had a strange accent—British, and yet not quite British. I moved back a step or two and he followed, keeping the distance between us constant.

"There is a fuel-dump valve located at the left of the water manifold," he said, in the same tone you might ask to have the sugar passed. "Open it."

I thought of things to say then, but the gun was the answer to all of them. I climbed down and found the valve and opened it; diesel fuel gushed out, making a soft splashing sound hitting the water on the port side. Three hundred gallons of number two, spreading out oily on the flat water.

"Open the forward scuttle valve," the man with the gun said.

He moved with me as I lifted the hatch, watched me open the valve to let the green water boil in. Then we went aft and opened the other one. The water made a cool, gurgling sound coming in. I could see it in the open engine hatch, rising beside the big cylinder blocks, with bits of flotsam swirling on the dark surface. In two minutes she was down by the stern, listing a little to port.

"It's a cumbersome way to commit suicide," I said. "Why not just go over the side?"

"Close the aft valve," he said. He was braced against the side of the cockpit, cool and calm, a technician doing his job. I wondered what the job might be, but I went aft fast and closed the valve. Then the forward one. By then, she was riding low, her gunwales about six inches out of the water. The smell of the oil was thick in the air.

"If the wind comes up, under we go," I said. "And with no fuel, that means no pumps—"

"Lie down on the deck," he cut me off.

I shook my head. "I'll take it standing up."

"As you wish." He dropped the gun muzzle and I tensed and shifted my weight to make my try and the gun made a sharp humming noise and liquid fire smashed into me and tore my flesh apart.

... I was lying with my face against the deck, quivering like a freshly amputated leg. I got my knees under me and got to my feet.

The man in the white uniform was gone. I was alone on the boat.

5

I went over her from bow to transom—not that I thought I'd find him hiding in the bait locker. It was just something to do while I got used to the idea of what had happened. I finished that and leaned against the deckhouse while a spell of pain-nausea passed. The spot I'd picked to ride out the night hours was sixty miles south of Key West, about forty north of the Castillo del Morro. I was afloat, as long as the wind didn't rise enough to put a riffle on the water. I had plenty of food, and water for two days—maybe three if I stretched it. The man with the gun had fixed my radio before he left; I checked and found a tube missing. There was no spare. That meant my one chance was to stay afloat until somebody happened past who could put a line on me. It would mean losing the boat—but she was as good as lost now, unless I could save her fast.

There wasn't much I could do in that direction: the hand pump in the bilge was under two feet of water. I spent an hour rerigging it on deck, and put in another hour working the handle before it broke. I may have lowered the level an eighth of an inch—or maybe it was just the light. I bailed for a while with a bait bucket, doing math in my head: at six buckets a minute, figuring three gallons to a bucket, how long to pour ten thousand gallons over the side? Too long, was the answer I came up with. By noon, the wind was starting to stir, and the level was down about an inch. I fished a canned ham and a bottle of beer out of the water sloshing around in the galley, then sat on the shady side of the cockpit and watched the pale clouds piling up far away across the brassy water, and thought about sitting in the cool dimness of Molly's bar, telling her about how a mysterious man in a dapper white suit had aimed something he called a nerve-gun at me and told me to dump her fuel and scuttle her, and then disappeared while I was lying down . . .

I got up and checked the spot where he'd been standing. There was nothing there to prove he hadn't been an illusion. He'd walked me forward, and then aft again, but that hadn't left a trail, either. I had opened the dump valve myself, flooded her myself. There was still the missing radio tube, but maybe I'd sneaked in and done that, too, while I wasn't looking. Maybe the hot tropical sun had finally crisped my brains, and the shot from the nerve-gun, which I could still feel every time I moved, had been the kind of fit people have after they've lost their grip on reality.

But I was just talking to myself. I knew what I'd seen. I remembered that hard, competent face, the way the light had glinted along the barrel of the gun, the incongruously spotless whites with the shiny lapel insignia with the letters TNL in blue enamel on them. I got my bucket and went back to work.

6

A breeze sprang up at sunset, and in ten minutes she had shipped more water than I had bailed in ten hours. She wallowed in the swells, logy as a gravid sea cow. She'd swamp sometime in the night, and I'd swim for a while, and after that. . . .

There wasn't any future in that line of thought. I

stretched out on my back on top of the deckhouse and closed my eyes and listened to her creak, as she moved in the water with all that weight in her. . . .

. . . And came awake, still listening, but to a new sound now. It was full dark, with no moon. I slid down to the deck and solid water came over the gunwale and soaked me to the knees.

I heard the sound again; it came from forward—a dull *thunk*! like something heavy bringing up solid against the decking. I reached down inside the cockpit and brought out the big six-cell flash I keep clamped to the wall beside the chart board and flicked it on and shone it up that way, and a voice out of the dark said, "Curlon—kill that light!"

I went flat against the house and flashed the beam along the rail and found his feet, raised it and put it square in his eyes. It wasn't the man who'd used the pain-gun on me. He was tall, gray-haired, wearing a trim gray coverall. His hands were empty.

"Put the light out," he said. "Quick! It's important!"

I switched off the flash. I could still see him faintly.

"There's no time to explain," he said. "You'll have to abandon her!"

"I don't suppose you brought a boat with you?" More water came over the side. She shuddered under me.

"Something better," he said. "But we'll have to make it fast. Come on forward!"

I didn't answer because I was halfway to him. I tried to find his silhouette against the sky, but it was all the same color.

"She's sinking fast," he said. "Jumping me won't change that."

"Her fuel and water tanks are dry," I said. "Maybe she'll float." I gained another yard.

"We don't have time to wait and see. There are only a few seconds left."

He was standing on the forehatch, half turned to the left, looking out into the dark as though there were something interesting out there he didn't want to miss. I followed the way he was looking and saw it.

It was a platform, about ten feet on a side, with a railing around it that reflected faint highlights from what looked like a glowing dish perched on a stand in the center. It was about a hundred yards away, drifting a few feet above the water. There were two men on it, both in the white suits. One of them was the man who'd scuttled my boat. The other was a little man with big ears: I couldn't see his face.

"What's the hurry?" I said. "I see a man I need to have a talk with."

"I can't force you," the man in gray said. "I can only tell you that this time they're holding all the cards. I'm offering you a chance at a new deal. Look!" He hooked a thumb over his shoulder. At first I didn't see anything; then I did: a rectangle, six feet high, two feet wide, like an open doorway into a room where a dim candle burned.

"I can't afford to be caught," the man in gray said. "Follow me—if you decide to trust me." He turned and stepped up into the ghost-door hanging in the air and was gone.

The platform was coming up fast now; the lean man was standing at the forward edge with the nerve-gun in his hand. "Give me ten seconds" I said to the hole in the air.

I went back along the pilot-house, dropped down into hip-deep water in the cockpit. I felt around up above the dead binnacle light, found the leather belt and sheath, strapped it on. As I swung back up. I felt her start to go. White water churned up around my waist, almost broke my grip on the rail. The glowing doorway was still there, hanging in the air six feet away. I jumped for it as she slid under. There was a sensation like needles against my skin as I crossed the line of light; then my feet struck floor, and I was standing in the strangest room I ever saw.

Chapter Two

It was about eight feet by ten, carpeted with curved white-painted walls lined with the glitter of screens, dials, instrument faces, more levers and gadgets than the cockpit of a Navy P2V. The man in gray was sitting in one of two contoured bucket seats in front of an array of colored lights. He flashed me a quick glance, hit a button at the same time. A soft humming sound started up; there was an indefinable sense of motion, in some medium other than space.

"Close, but I don't think they saw us," he said tensely. "At least there's no tac-ray on us. But we have to move out fast, before he sets up a full-scale scan pattern." He was looking into a small, green-glowing screen, the size of a flight-deck radarscope, flipping levers at the same time. The scanning line swept down from top to bottom, about two cycles per second. I'd never seen one like it. But then I'd never seen anything like any of what had happened in the last few minutes.

"Who are they?" I said. "What are they?"

He gave me a fast up-and-down look. "For the moment, suffice it to say they're representatives of someone who seems to have taken a dislike to you." He flipped a switch and the lights dimmed down almost to nothing. On a big screen, six feet square, a picture snapped into sharp focus. It was the platform, hovering above the choppy water about fifty feet away, receding. The view was as clear as though I were looking out through a picture window. One of the men in white was playing a powerful beam of bluish light across the waves. My boat was gone. There was nothing in sight but a few odds and ends of gear, bobbing on the black water.

"You dropped off his tracer cold," the man in gray said. "He won't like that very well—but it couldn't be helped. By picking you up, I've put myself in what one might call an impossible position." He eyed me as if he were thinking over how much more to tell me.

"After what's already happened, that's not a word I'd use lightly," I said. "What are you—FBI? CIA? Not that they'd have anything like this." I nodded at that fantastic control panel.

"My name is Bayard," he said. "I'm afraid you're going to have to take me on trust for a while, Mr. Curlon."

"How do you know my name?"

"I've been following them," he nodded at the screen. "I've learned a number of things about you."

"Why did you pick me up?"

"Curiosity is as good a word as any."

"If you were tailing them, how did you manage to get here first?"

"I extrapolated their route and got ahead of them. I was lucky; I spotted you in time."

"How? It's a dark night, and I was showing no lights."

"I used an instrument which responds to . . . certain characteristics of matter."

"Make that a little plainer, will you, Bayard?"

"I'm not being intentionally mysterious," he said. "But there are regulations."

"Whose regulations?"

"I can't tell you that."

"So I just ask you to drop me at the next corner, and go on home and have a couple of drinks as if nothing had happened. By tomorrow the whole thing will seem silly—except for my boat."

He stared at the screen. "No, you can't do that, of course." He gave me a sharp stare. "Are you sure you're not holding something back? Something that would shed some light on all this?"

"You're the man of mystery, not me. I'm just a fisherman—or was until today."

"Not just any fisherman. A fisherman named Richard Henry Geoffrey Edward Curlon."

"I didn't think there was anyone alive who knew I had three middle initials."

"He knows. He also knows something that makes you important enough to be the object of a full-scale Net operation. I'd like to know what it is."

"It must be a case of mistaken identity. There's nothing about me to interest anyone except a specialist in hard-luck cases."

Bayard frowned at me. "Do you mind if I run a few tests on you? It will only take a minute or two. Nothing unpleasant."

"That will be a nice change," I said. "What kind of tests, for what purpose?"

"To find out what it is about you that interests them," he nodded at the screen. "I'll tell you the results—if any." He took out a gadget and ran it over me like a photographer checking light levels.

"If the word hadn't already been overworked," he said, "I'll call these readings impossible." He pointed to a green needle that wavered, hunting around a luminous dial, like a compass at the North Pole. "According to this, you're in an infinite number of places at the same time. And this one—" he indicated a smaller dial with a glowing yellow arrow, "says that the energy levels concentrated in your area are of the order of ten thousand percent of normal."

"Your wires are crossed," I suggested.

"Apparently," he went on thinking out loud, "you represent a nexus point in what is known as a probability stress pattern. Unless I miss my guess, a major nexus."

"Meaning what?"

"That great affairs hinge on you, Mr. Curlon. What, or

how, I don't know. But strange things are happening—and you're at the center of them. What you do next could have a profound effect on the future of the world—of many worlds."

"Slow down," I said. "Let's stick to reality."

"There is more than one reality, Mr. Curlon," Bayard said flatly.

"Who did you say you were again?" I asked him.

"Bayard. Colonel Brion Bayard of Imperial Intelligence."

"Intelligence, eh? And Imperial at that. Sounds a little old-fashioned—unless you're working for Haile Selassie."

"The Imperium is a great power, Mr. Curlon. But please accept my word that my government is not inimicable to yours."

"Nowadays, that's something. How is it you speak American without an accent?"

"I was born in Ohio. But let's leave that aside for the moment. I've bought some time by whisking you out from under his nose, but he won't give up. And he has vast resources at his disposal." I still had the feeling he was talking to himself.

"All right, you've bought time," I prompted him. "What are you going to do with it?"

Bayard pointed to a dial with a slim red needle that trembled over a compass face. "This instrument is capable of tracing relationships of a high order of abstraction. Given a point of fixure, it indicates the position of artifacts closely associated with the subject. At the moment, it indicates a distant source, to the east of our present position."

"Science, Mr. Bayard? Or witchcraft?"

"The wider science ranges, the more it impinges on the area of what was once known as the occult. But after all, occult merely means hidden."

"What does all this have to do with me?"

"The instrument is attuned to you, Mr. Curlon. If we

follow it, it may lead us to the answers to your questions and mine."

"And when we get there—then what?"

"That depends on what we find."

"You don't give away much, do you, Colonel?" I said. "I've had a long day. I appreciate your picking me off my boat before she went under—and I suppose I owe you some thanks for saving me from another taste of Mr. Renata's nerve-gun. But the question-and-no-answer game is wearing me down."

"Let's reach an understanding, Mr. Curlon," Bayard said. "If I could explain, you'd understand—but the explanation would involve telling you the things I can't tell you."

"We're talking in circles, Colonel. I suppose you know that."

"The circle is tightening, Mr. Curlon. I'm hoping it isn't a noose that will choke us all."

"That's pretty dramatic language, isn't it, Colonel? You make it sound like the end of the world."

Bayard nodded, holding my eyes. In the varicolored light from the instrument panel, his face was hard, set in lines of tension.

"Precisely, Mr. Curlon," he said.

2

The moon rose, painting a silver highway across the water. We bypassed Bermuda, saw the lights of the Azores in the distance. Two more hours passed, while the ocean unrolled under us, until the shore of France came into view dead ahead.

"The proximity sensors are registering in the beta range now," Bayard said. "We're within a few miles of what we're looking for."

He moved a lever and the moonlit curve of the shore dropped away under us. It was swift, noiseless, smooth. We leveled off at a height of a couple of hundred feet over tilled fields, swung over the tiled rooftops of a small village, followed a narrow, winding road that cut through a range of wooded hills. Far ahead, a wide river glittered against the black land.

"The Seine," Bayard said. He studied the illuminated chart that unrolled on a small screen before him, with a red dot in the center that represented our position.

"The indicator is reading in the red now. Not much farther."

Ahead, the river curved between high banks. At the widest point, there was a steep, tree-covered island.

"Does any of this look familiar to you?" Bayard asked. "Have you ever been here before?"

"No. It doesn't look like much. A river, and an island."

"Not just an island, Mr. Curlon," Bayard said. "Take a closer look." There was a note of suppressed excitement in his voice.

"There's a building," I said. I could make it out now: a massive pile of stone, topped by castellated towers.

"A rather famous building—known as Château Gaillard," Bayard said. He glanced at me. "Does the name mean anything to you?"

"I've heard of it. Pretty old, isn't it?"

"About eight hundred years." All the while we talked, the shuttle was gliding in across the river, toward the stone walls and towers of the fortress. Bayard adjusted levers and we stopped, hanging in empty air about fifty feet from the face of the high wall. There was ivy growing there, and in the spaces between the dark leaves the stone looked as old as the rocks below.

"We're within five hundred feet of the center of resonance." Bayard said. "It's somewhere below us." The wall in front of us slid upward as the shuttle dropped vertically. There were narrow loopholes in the stonework, between weathered buttresses that gripped the rockface like talons. We leveled off at the base of the wall.

"Our target is some twelve feet below this point, and approximately sixteen feet to the north-northeast," Bayard said.

"That puts it somewhere in the foundations," I said. "It seems we're out of luck."

"You're about to have another unusual experience, Mr. Curlon," Bayard said. "Hold on to your equanimity." He flipped a switch. The view on the screen faded into a sort of luminous blue, the color of a gas flame, and about as solid-looking. He moved the controls, and the ghost-wall slid upward. The line of rubble that was the surface slid past, like water rising over a periscope, and the screen went solid blue, with clearly defined stratum lines running across it at an angle. There were a few embedded stones, a darker shade of blue, like lumps of gelatin floating in an aquarium, some gnarled roots, pale and transparent, pieces of broken pottery. The screen went darker, almost opaque.

"We're into the solid rock now," Bayard said in a tone as calm as if he were pointing out movie stars' homes. We stopped, and I felt a few million tons of the planet pushing in at me. It gave me a strange, insubstantial feeling, as if I were nothing but a pattern drawn in smoke, like the gaseous granite just beyond the thin hull.

"As I said, quite a machine," I grunted. "What else will she do?"

Bayard showed me a faint smile and touched the controls. The texture of the rock swirled around us like muddy water with a dim light shining through it. We eased forward about ten feet, and slid out through a wall and were in a small room, stone walled and floored, windowless, thick with dust. It was almost bright here, after the trip through the rock. There were things in the room: the tattered shreds of a rotted tapestry on the wall, a wooden bench, crudely made from rough planks, heaped with dust; some metal plates and mugs ornately decorated with colored stones, pieces of gaudy jewelry, lumps of rusted iron.

"I think maybe we've found something, Mr. Curlon," Bayard said, and now he didn't sound quite so calm. "Shall we step out and have a closer look?"

3

Bayard did things with his levers and a soft hum I'd forgotten I was hearing ran down the scale, and the scene on the viewplate faded, as if a projector had been switched off. He snapped another switch and a harsh white light glared against the bleak walls, casting black shadows in the corners. The panel slid back and I stepped out after him. The dust was a soft carpet underfoot; the odor of age in the air was like all the musty books in all the forgotten libraries.

"An old storeroom," Bayard said in the kind of hushed voice that went with a disturbed grave. "Sealed up, probably centuries ago."

"It could do with a sweeping," I said.

"The cloth and wood and leather have rotted away, except for the heavier pieces. And most of the metal has oxidized."

I stirred a heap of rust with my foot. A flake the size of a saucer crumbled off. Bayard went to one knee, poked at the corrosion, lifted the curved piece clear.

"This is a *genouillère*," he said. "A knee guard; part of a suit of chain armor."

He had an instrument like a Geiger counter in his hand, with a pointer on a cable that he aimed around the room.

"There are extraordinary forces at work here," he said. "The Net tension reading is off the end of the scale."

"Meaning?"

"The fabric of reality is stretched to the breaking point. It's almost as if there were a discontinuity in the continuum—a break in the entropic sequence. Forces like these can't exist, Mr. Curlon—not for long—not without neutralization!"

He changed the settings on the gadget he was holding, swung around to point it at me.

"You seem to represent the focus of a strongly polarized energy flow," he said. He came closer, pointed the instrument at my face, waved it down across my chest, stopped with the thing aimed at my left hip.

"The knife," he said. "May I see it?"

I took it out and handed it over. It was nothing much to look at: a wide, thick blade, about a foot long, ground to a rather crude point, with a stubby cross-guard and an oversized, leather-wrapped handle. It wasn't the handiest scaling knive in the world, but I'd had it a long time. Bayard held the metal pointer against it and looked incredulous.

"Where did you get this, Mr. Curlon?"

"I found it."

"Where?"

"In a trunk, in an attic, a long time ago."

"Whose trunk? Whose attic? Think carefully, Mr. Curlon. This may be of vital importance."

"It was my grandfather's attic, the day after he died. The trunk had been in the family a long time; the story was it belonged to a sea-faring ancestor, back in the eighteen hundreds. I was rummaging in it and turned the knife up. I kept it. I don't know why. It's not much, as knives go, but it seemed to fit my hand pretty well."

Bayard looked closely at the blade. "There's lettering here," he said. "It looks like Old French: *Dieu et mon droit.*"

"We didn't come all this way just to study my knife," I said.

"Why keep calling it a knife, Mr. Curlon?" Bayard said. "We both know better." He gripped the hilt of the weapon and hefted it. "It's much too massive for a knife, too clumsy."

"What would you call it?"

"It's a broken sword, Mr. Curlon. Didn't you know?"

He offered it to me, hilt first. As I took it, Bayard looked at his dials. "The reading went up into the blue when you took it in your hand," he said in a voice that was as taut as a tow-cable.

In my hand, the hilt of the knife seemed to tingle. It tugged, gently, as if invisible fingers were pulling at it. Bayard was watching my face. I felt sweat trickle down across my left eyebrow. Hackles I didn't know I had were trying to rise. I took a step and the pull became stronger. A vivid blue spark, like static electricity, played across a lump of rusted iron on the bench. Another step, and a faint blue halo sprang up around the end of the knife. From the corner of my eye, I saw that objects all around the room were glowing softly in the gloom. Dust trickled from the bench; something stirred there, rotated a few inches, stopped. I took a step sideways; it pivoted, following me.

Bayard stirred the dust with his finger, lifted a piece of pitted steel about three inches by six, beveled along both edges, with a groove along the central ridge.

"Just a piece of scrap iron," I said. "What made it move?"

"Unless I'm mistaken, Mr. Curlon," Bayard said, "it's a piece of your broken sword."

Chapter Three

"I don't believe in magic, Colonel," I said.

"Not magic," Bayard said. "There are subtle relationships between objects, Mr. Curlon; affinities between people and the inanimates that play a role in their lives."

"It's just old iron, Bayard. Nothing else."

"Objects are a part of their environment," Bayard said flatly. "Every quantum of matter-energy in this Universe has been here since its inception. The atoms that make up this blade were formed before the sun was formed; they were there, in the rock, when the first life stirred in the seas. Then the metal was mined, smelted, forged. But always, the matter itself has been a part of the immutable sum total of this material plane of reality. Complex interrelationships exist among the particles of a given worldline—relationships which are affected by the uses to which the matter they comprise are put. Such a relationship exists between you and this ancient weapon."

Bayard was grinning now—the grin of an old gray wolf who smells blood. "I'm beginning to put two and two together: you—with that red mane, that physique—and now this. Yes, I think I'm beginning to understand who you are, Mr. Curlon—*what* you are."

"And what am I?"

Bayard made a motion that took in the room, and the massive pile above it. "This chateau was built in the year 1196 by an English king," he said. "His name was Richard—known as the Lion-Hearted."

"That's what *he* was. What am I?"

"You're his descendant, Mr. Curlon. The last of the Plantagenets."

2

I laughed aloud at the letdown. "I suppose the next move is to offer me a genuine hand-painted reconstruction of the family coat of arms, suitable for framing. This must be your idea of humor, Colonel. And even if it were true, after thirty generations, any connection between him and a modern descendant would be statistically negligible."

"Careful, Mr. Curlon; your education is showing," Bayard's smile was grim. "Your information is correct—as far as it goes. But a human being is more than a statistical complex. There are linkages, Mr. Curlon—relationships that go beyond Mendel and Darwin. The hand of the past still reaches out to mold the present—and the future—"

"I see. The lad with the nerve-gun is running me down to collect a bill that Richard the First owed his tailor—"

"Bear with me a moment, Mr. Curlon. Accept the fact that reality is more complex than the approximations that science calls the axioms of physics. Every human action has repercussions that spread out across a vast continuum. Those repercussions can have profound effects—effects beyond your present conception of the exocosm. You're not finished with all this yet. You're involved—inevitably, like it or not. You have enemies, Mr. Curlon; enemies capable of aborting every undertaking you attempt. And I'm beginning to get a glimmering of an idea why that might be."

"I'll admit somebody sank my boat," I said. "But that's all. I don't believe in vast plots, aimed at me."

"Don't be too sure, Mr. Curlon. When I discovered that missions were being carried out in B-I Three—the official designation of this area—I looked into the matter. Some of those missions were recent—within the last few weeks. But others dated back over a period of almost thirty years."

"Which means someone has been after me since I was a year old? I ask you, Colonel: Is that reasonable?"

"Nothing about this affair is reasonable, Mr. Curlon. Among other curiosa is that fact that the existence of B-I Three wasn't officially known to Intelligence HQ until ten years ago—" He broke off, shook his head as though irritated. "I realize that everything I say only compounds your confusion—"

"Am I the one who's confused, Colonel?"

"Everything that's happened has a meaning—is a part of a pattern. We must discover what that pattern is, Mr. Curlon."

"All this, on the basis of a fishknife and a piece of rusty metal?"

I put out my hand and he put the piece of iron in it. The upper end was broken in a shallow V. There was a gentle tugging, as if the two pieces of metal were trying to orient themselves in relation to each other.

"If it's all my imagination, Mr. Curlon," Bayard said softly, "why are you fighting to hold the two pieces apart?"

I let the smaller shard turn, brought it slowly across toward the point of the knife. When it was six inches away, a long pink spark jumped across the gap. The pull increased. I tried to hold them apart, but it was no use. They moved together and touched . . . and a million volts of lightning smashed down and lit the room with a blinding glare.

3

The rays of the late sun shone fitfully from a cloud-serried sky, and shadows fled across the sward, across the faces of those who stood before me, swelled up in arrogance, petty men who would summon a king to an accounting. One stood forth among them, a-glitter in rich stuff, and made much of flourishing the scrolls from which he spelled out those demands by which they thought to bind my royal power.

To the end I let him speak his treason, for all to hear. Then I gave my answer.

From the dark forest roundabout my picked archers stepped forth, and in a dread silence bent their bows. And my heart sang as their shafts sang, finding their marks in traitors' breasts. And under my eyes were the false barons slain, every one, and when the deed was done I walked forth from my pavilion and looked on their dead faces and spurned with my foot that scrap of parchment they called their Charter.

4

The voices and the faces faded. The shadowed walls of the old storeroom closed in around me. But it was as though years had passed, and the room was a forgotten memory from some distant life, lived long ago.

"What happened?" Bayard's voice rasped in the silence.

"I . . . know not," I heard myself say, and my own voice sounded strange in my ears. " 'Twas some fit took hold on me." I made an effort and shook the last of the fog out of my brain. Bayard was pointing at me—at what I held in my hand.

"My God, the sword!"

I looked—and felt time stop while my pulse boomed in my ears. The broken blade, which had been a foot long, was half again that length now. The two pieces of metal had welded themselves together into a single unit.

5

"The seam of the joining is invisible," Bayard said. "It's as though the two parts had never been separated."

I ran my fingers over the dark metal. The color, the pattern of oxidation was unbroken.

"What did you experience while it was happening?" Bayard asked.

"Dreams. Visions."

"What kind of visions?"

"Not pleasant ones."

Bayard's eyes went past me to the wall beyond.

"The sword wasn't the only thing that was affected," he said in a tight voice. "Look!"

I looked. Against the stones, where only tatters had been, a faded tapestry hung. It showed a dim, crudely worked design of huntsmen and hounds. There was nothing remarkable about it—except that it hadn't been there five minutes ago.

"Notice the pattern," Bayard said. "The big figure in the center is wearing a cloak trimmed in ermine tails—a symbol of royalty. My guess is that's Richard himself." He looked around the room, bent and picked up the *genouillère*. The metal was dark with age, but there was no rust on it now.

"What happened here had an effect on the fabric of the continuum itself," Bayard said. "Reality is being reshaped as the Net tensions resolve themselves. There are fantastic powers in balance, Mr. Curlon, ready for a touch to send them tumbling one way—or another." His eyes held on mine. "Someone is working to upset that balance. I think we can take it as axiomatic that we must oppose him."

As he finished speaking, a bell clanged from the shuttle. Bayard leaped to the panel, hit the switches.

"There's a tracer locked on us at close range!" he snapped. "They followed us here! The energy discharge must have given them a fix to home on." The familiar humming sound started up, but this time it had a groaning note, as if it was working under an overload. I smelled hot insulation, and smoke curled up from behind the panel.

"Too late," Bayard said. "He's holding a suppressor

beam on us. We can't shift out of identity with this line. It looks like we're trapped!"

A deep thrumming sound started up somewhere. I could feel it vibrating through the floor of the room. Dust floated from the cracks in the walls, rose from the floor. A metal ornament made a soft thump falling off the bench.

"He's right above us," Bayard said. "He doesn't have half-phase capability; he'll use a force probe to dig his way down to us."

"All right," I said. "Let him. Two against two is fair odds."

"I can't take the chance," Bayard said. "It's not just you and me—it's this machine. It's unique, a special model. And if what I'm beginning to suspect is true, letting it fall into Renata's hands would be a major disaster."

"Renata?" I started to ask all the questions, but Bayard pulled a ring from his finger, handed it to me. "This is a control device governing the half-phase unit. With it, you can hold the machine clear until he's gone. You'll know, when the red light goes off—"

"Where will you be?"

"I'll meet him, try to steer him away from you. If he has any suspicion of what's happened, he'll be able to detect the shuttle, and grapple it."

"I'll stay, Bayard," I said. "I have a bone to pick with Mr. Renata."

"No—there's no time to argue! Do as I ask, Curlon, or he'll take both of us!" He didn't wait for an answer; he stepped out of the shuttle and the entry snapped shut behind him. His image appeared on the screen.

"Now, Mr. Curlon!" his voice came through the speaker. "Or it will be too late for both of us!"

A crack had already appeared in the wall he was facing. The time for talk had all run out. I pressed the stone set in the ring and heard a soft *click*! and felt space twist between my bones.

33

6

A soft, high-pitched whine started up, went up and off into the supersonic. Bayard's outline turned transparent blue, like the wall behind him. To him, the shuttle was invisible now.

"Good man," he said. His voice had a whispery quality but it was clear enough. He turned and faced the wall. A section of it bulged and fell in. A beam of dazzling light played through the opening. A man stepped through. It was Renata, the foxy man I'd left unconscious on the dock at Key West a couple of short lifetimes ago; there was no doubt about it: the sharp eyes, the narrow jaw, the slick black hair. But now he was in a swank white uniform that he wore as if he'd been born to it. But it was his face that bothered me most. I'd hit him hard, but there was no mark on him to prove it. He looked around the room, then at Bayard.

"You seem to be a long way from home, Colonel," he said, in a casual drawling voice—nothing like Renata's throaty whine.

"About the same as you, Major," Bayard said.

"Why did you come here—to this particular spot? And how did you get in? I see no entrance from the outside—other than the one I used."

Bayard glanced at the broken wall. "Your tactics seem a little rough for use in an interdicted area, Major. Are you acting on orders—or have you gone in business for yourself?"

"I'm afraid for the present you'll answer the questions, Colonel. You're under arrest, of course. Where have you left your shuttle?"

"I lent it to a friend."

"Don't fence with me, Bayard. It dropped completely off my screens less than half a minute ago—just as it did earlier, in the Gulf of Mexico. It seems you have equipment in your possession unknown to Imperial Intelligence. I shall have to ask you to lead me to it."

"I can't help you."

"You realize I must use force, if necessary. I can't permit the subject Curlon to slip out of my hands."

"I'm afraid you already have."

The little man half turned his head. "Lujac," he called. Another man came in through the hole in the wall. It was the fellow who'd used the nerve-gun on me. He had it in his hand now.

"Level three," the major said. Lujac raised the gun and pressed the firing stud on the side. Bayard staggered and doubled over.

"Enough," the little man said.

"Colonel, you're in considerable difficulty: absence from your post of duty without leave, interference with an official Net operation, and so on. All this will be dealt with in due course—but if you'll cooperate with me now, I think I can promise to make it easier for you."

"You don't know . . . what you're doing," Bayard got the words out. It wasn't easy; I knew what he was going through then. "There are forces . . . involved . . ."

"Never mind what's involved," the major snapped. "I don't mean to let the man slip through my fingers. Speak up, now! How did you do it? Where is he hidden?"

"You're wasting . . . your breath," Bayard said. "You know damned well you can't break my conditioning. Face it, Major; he got away from you. What are you going to do about it?"

"Don't be a fool, Bayard! You know the Imperium faces a crisis—and you're well aware that I'm acting on orders from a very high ranking official! You're throwing away not only your career, but your life, if you oppose me! Now—I want an explanation of why you came to this spot, what you expected to accomplish here—and where you've sent the man I want!"

"I'll bet you do," Bayard said. "Try and get it."

35

"Let me deal with the swine," Lujac said, and took a quick step forward, but Renata waved him back.

"I'm taking you in to Stockholm Zero-zero," he told Bayard. "You'll face a firing squad for this night's work—I promise you that!" He put cuffs on him and they went out through the hole in the wall. Half a minute later the red telltale light went off, meaning Renata's shuttle was gone. I flipped the switch that shifted me back to full-phase identity, waited for the color to come back into things, then stepped out and switched the machine back to half-phase. It shimmered like a mirage and winked out. The air was still swirling from that when the tunnel mouth exploded. When the dust cleared, it was packed solid with broken rock. The major had taken the precaution of closing the route behind him.

Chapter Four

It took me four hours of shifting sharp-edged rock fragments before I pushed aside the last slab and poked my head out into the open air beside the old stone wall rising up from a tangle of untrimmed shrubbery. I climbed out and breathed some fresh night air and tried to shake off the feeling that I was dreaming the whole thing. The Occam principle told me that the simplest explanation was that I was strapped into a jacket in some quiet rest home, living out a full-fledged delusional system. But if I was dreaming it, the dream was still on. Ten feet from the hole I'd crawled out of, I found a set of booted footprints which led a few yards to the imprint of a set of skids. That would be where the major's shuttle had been parked—if there had been a major, and he had a shuttle, and it had been parked.

And while I was still following that one through, I got the proof I'd been wanting: The man called Lujac stepped out from black shadows and for the second time I felt the bone-crushing agony of the nerve-gun sweep over me.

2

I came to lying on the floor in front of the control panel of a shuttle with my arms clamped behind me. It wasn't Bayard's machine, but there was no mistaking the sweep of unfamiliar dials and the big pink-glowing screen, or the hum that went between my bones until it rose out of the audible range. On the screen, things were happening. The old walls rising on the left of the screen flickered and sank down into heaps of rubble, with weeds poking out from between the stone slabs. The weeds withered and the rubble blackened into cokelike ash, then glowed blue and slumped into puddled lava. The river was rising, it welled out over its banks and became an oily black sea that stretched away to a row of volcanic cones that shed red light on the far horizon. Green slime crawled up on the rocks that showed above the surface. It changed into moss that grew into toadstools fifty feet high that jostled and thrust for footing. The water receded, and new plants swarmed up out of the sea; a vine-thing like writhing snakes threw itself over the jungle and tiny black plants sprang up along its tendrils, eating at it like acid. Broad leaves poked out from under the rotted vegetation and wrapped themselves around the black vine-eaters. I saw all this through a sort of purple haze of pain that did nothing to brighten the nightmare.

Animal life appeared: Strange creatures with deformed limbs and misshapen bodies like melting wax statues posed among the cancerous plants. The leaves grew huge and curled and fell away, and scaly, deformed trees rose up, and all the while the creatures didn't move. They swelled, twisted, flowed into new shapes. A forty-foot lizard was locked in the clutch of a plant with rubbery, spike-studded branches that wound around the bossed hide until the hide grew its own spikes that impaled the thorn tree, and it shriveled and fell away and the lizard dwindled into a crouching frog-thing that bloated into a stranded tadpole the size of a cow and sank into the ooze.

For a while, night glowed like day under a radioactive moon; and then the ground dissolved and the shuttle was hanging in black space, with the glare of the sun coming from behind to illuminate the undersides of the dust and rock fragments that arched up and over in a pale halo that must have dwarfed Saturn's rings. Then land appeared again: a dusty plain where small plants sprouted and grew thicker and turned into tangled underbrush dotted with small, cancerous trees. They grew taller and developed normal bark and green leaves, and slowly the atmosphere cleared and the moon was riding high and white in a dark sky full of luminous clouds.

Lujac switched off and the sound of the drive dwindled down to a low growl and died. He pointed the nerve-gun at me, gestured toward the exit. I made it to my feet, stepped out onto a trimmed green lawn beside a high stone wall that was the same one we'd started from. But now there was ivy growing there, and lighted windows, up high. There were flowerbeds along the base, and a tended path led off down the slope toward the moonlit water of the river below. The trees were gone, but other trees grew in places where there had been no trees. Across the river, the lights of a town glowed, not quite where the town had been before.

We went along the path to a broad, paved walk, rounded the front of the building. Light blazed from a wide entry with glass doors set in the old stone. Two sharp-looking troopers in white jodhpurs snapped to and passed us into a high marble hall. Nobody seemed to think there was anything exceptional about a prisoner in cuffs being gunwalked here. We went along a corridor to an office where neat secretaries sat at typewriters with only three rows of keys. A lean, worried-looking man exchanged a few words with Lujac, and passed us into an inner office where Major Renata sat at a desk, talking into a recorder microphone. He twitched his sharp mouth into a foxy smile when he saw me and motioned Lujac out of the room.

This wasn't the same man I'd known back in Key West, I saw that now. It was his twin brother, better fed, better bred, but with the same kind of mind behind the same sly face. Not a man I'd ever really take a liking to.

"You led me quite a chase, Mr. Curlon," he said. "It's unfortunate that events fell out as they did; I had hoped to handle matters more subtly. You understand that I require certain information from you as the first order of business. Let's begin with the matter of Colonel Bayard's involvement. When did he first contact you, and what was his proposition?"

"Where is he now?"

"Never mind that!" Renata rapped. "Don't be confused by any false sense of misguided loyalty, Mr. Curlon. You owe him nothing! Now—answer my questions fully and promptly, and I give you my assurance that you will be in no way held accountable for his crimes."

"Why did you sink my boat?"

"It was necessary. You will be reimbursed, Mr. Curlon. As a matter of fact, you are an extremely lucky man. When this matter is finished up to the satisfaction of, ah, Imperial authorities, you'll find yourself in a most comfortable situation for the rest of your life."

"Why me?"

"I'm acting on instructions, Mr. Curlon. As to precisely why you were selected for this opportunity, I can't say. Merely accept your good fortune and give me your cooperation. Now, kindly begin by telling me precisely how Bayard contacted you and what he told you of his plans."

"Why not ask him?"

"Mr. Curlon, please limit your comments to answering questions for the present. Later, all your questions will be answered—within the limits of Imperial security requirements, of course."

I nodded. I was in no hurry. What came next probably wouldn't be as much fun.

"I know about your good intentions," I said. "I've met your lieutenant, the fellow with the nerve-gun."

"It was necessary to insure there'd be no unfortunate accident, Mr. Curlon. You're a powerful man, possibly excessively combative. There was no time for explanations. And you've suffered no permanent injury. Oh, by the way: where did Bayard secrete the shuttle?"

"You mean the amphibious car he picked me up in?"

"Yes. It's Imperial property, of course. By helping me to recover it, you'll be reducing the charges against Bayard."

"He must have parked it out of sight."

"Mr. Curlon..." Renata's face tightened. "Perhaps you don't understand the seriousness of your situation. Cooperate, and your rewards will be great. Fail to cooperate, and you'll live to regret it."

"It seems you're always offering me a proposition, and I'm always turning it down," I said. "Maybe you and I just weren't meant to get together, Renata."

He took a breath as though he were about to yell, but instead he thumbed a button on his desk, savagely. The door opened and a couple of the armed troops were there.

"Place this subject in a Class Three quarters, MS block," he snapped. He favored me with a look like a poison dart. "Perhaps a few days of solitary contemplation will assist you in seeing the proper course," he snapped, and went back to his paper work.

3

They marched me along halls, down steps into less ornately decorated halls, down more steps, along a passage with no pretensions of elegance at all, stopped before a heavy iron-bound door. A boy with blond fuzz on his chin opened up. I stepped through into the dim light of a shielded bulb and the door closed behind me with a solid sound. I looked around and put my head back and laughed.

I was back in the underground room I'd started from all those hours before.

4

It was the same, and yet not quite the same. The floor was swept, and the litter of dust and rusty junk was gone. But the tapestry was still on the wall, more complete now than it had been.

I prowled around the room, but aside from a chair and a cot, I didn't find anything that hadn't been there before. I rapped on the walls, but no sliding panels opened up on hidden stairways with daylight showing at the top of them. I looked at the tapestry, but it didn't tell me anything. The central figure was a tall, red-bearded man with a bow slung at his back, a sword at his side. His horse was pawing the air with one hoof and the hounds were leaping up, as if they were eager to be off. I knew how they felt. I was ready to travel myself. But this time there was no convenient tunnel waiting to be dug out. It was too bad Renata hadn't tossed Bayard in the same VIP cell. Maybe he'd have had another trick ring up his sleeve. I looked at the one wedged on my little finger and felt a prickling along my scalp line at the thoughts I was thinking. I wondered if I was missing some angle that was too obvious to see, but if I was, it was still invisible.

I pushed the stone and got ready for nothing to happen. For five seconds, nothing did. Then air *whooshed* around me and the shuttle winked into existence, with the door open and the soft light gleaming from inside.

5

I stepped into the shuttle and sat in the chair facing all those dials, packed in the panel like chrome and glass anchovies. I tried to remember which ones Bayard had used, and a trickle of sweat went down the side of my face when I thought about all the things that could go wrong if I made a mistake. But thinking at a time like this was a mistake. It would be too bad if I cross-controlled and stalled out in the middle of the solid rock, but chances like this didn't come along every day. I pushed the half-phase switch and the walls faded to electric blue. The first lever I pushed did nothing that was visible. I worked another one and had a short heart attack when the shuttle started to sink through the floor. I moved it the other way and moved up like a balloon rising through dense blue fog. Seconds later, I popped through the surface. I was behind a dense clump of trees, just a few feet from the spot where I'd seen the runner-marks. Just a few feet, and at the same time, in some way I wasn't ready to try to put into words yet, as far away as you could get. And that brought me to the question of my next move.

For the moment, I was in the clear. If my operating the shuttle had registered on any meters in the vicinity, it wasn't apparent. The obvious thing for me to do was to return the machine to half-phase, get off the premises as fast as I could, and forget about a stranger named Bayard and his story of a probability crisis coming that would turn the world into bubbling chaos.

On the other hand, I was sitting on a device which, according to its previous owner, was something out of the ordinary, even among the men in the white Imperial uniforms. And those same high-powered operators owed me a few things, including one boat of which I'd been rather fond. I had an advantage now; they didn't know where the shuttle was, where I was. And I could watch them, without being seen.

There was just one catch: It meant operating a machine that was more sophisticated than a jet fighter, and potentially more dangerous. I'd watched Bayard at the controls; I had a rough idea of how he had maneuvered it. The big white lever marked DR-MAIN was the one that started everything working. It had a nice feel to it under my hand: smooth and cool, a lever that wanted to be pulled.

I was still sitting there, looking into the screen and thinking these thoughts when lights came on over a side entry fifty feet along the wall. The door opened and Major Renata stepped out, carrying a briefcase and talking over his shoulder to a harassed-looking adjutant with a notebook. My reaction was automatic: I punched the half-phase switch and the scene faded out to the transparent blue that meant I was invisible.

A big, boxy staff-car pulled up along the drive and Renata and four others got in and the car pulled away. I remembered the controls Bayard had used to maneuver on half-phase. I tried them; the shuttle glided away as smoothly as oil spreading out on water. I followed the car down the winding drive through parklike grounds, past a gate where a sentry yawned as I slid by two feet from him, across a bridge and through the village. On the open highway, he opened up, but I had no trouble staying with him.

6

I trailed the car for half an hour, until it pulled through a gate in a wire fence around a small grassed airstrip. Renata got out and his aides scuttled around, readying a big, fabric-covered prop-driven airplane with wings the size of barn roofs. There were handshakes and some heel-clicking from a couple of Germanic-looking fellows; then Renata and one other climbed in and the plane taxied out and headed into the wind.

I'd spent the time looking over the controls, and was ready when the plane revved up and started its run. It took me three tries to match my rate of ascent to the airplane's, but I managed it, then maneuvered into a spot a quarter of a mile astern. So far, it had been easy; all I'd had to do was steer. For all I knew, the instruments were indicating ten different critical overloads, but I'd worry about that when I had to. The theory of a shuttle was a complex thing, but straight-line operation was simple enough.

It was a three-hour flight over rolling farmland straight into the rising sun, then out across water that had to be the English Channel. The plane began letting down toward a city that had to be London, circled a field a few miles out from the center of the city, landed and taxied up to a small operations building with RBAF-NORTHOLT lettered across it. I had a bad few seconds when the pavement washed up around me like muddy water, but I managed to level the shuttle out a foot above the pavement.

Renata climbed down, and a car pulled out and collected him. By now I was getting used to the capabilities of my little machine; I didn't bother with the gate, just slid across through the fence and fell in behind the car as it picked up speed along a broad parkway that led straight toward the towers of the city.

It was a fast twenty-minute trip. Renata's car, with a few touches of a siren that sounded like a ghost wailing through the audio pickup, cleared traffic, making speed through narrow, twisting streets, crossed the Thames on a bridge with a fine view of the House of Commons, swung into a stone-walled courtyard behind a big, grim fortress. Renata stepped out and headed for a small door under a big wrought-iron lantern, and I followed him through the wall. The sun winked out and I was in a wide, well-lit corridor lined with open doors where people in uniform did what people do in government offices. Renata took a sudden corner, and I overcorrected, found myself in solid rock that must have been five feet thick. By the time I'd manuvered back into the open, he was out of sight.

For the next hour, I cruised through the building like a mechanized ghost, looking into big offices with ranks of filing cabinets and desks under banks of flourescents, into smaller offices with deep carpets and solemn-looking bureaucrats admiring their reflections in the picture windows, into storerooms, a message center. I tried the lower levels, found dead-record storage, a mechanical equipment room, a small theater, and lower still, some grim-looking cells. There was nothing for me there. I took a shortcut through a wall and was in an eight-foot-square room with rusty manacles and a hole in the floor for plumbing. It had everything a medieval dungeon needed except a couple of human skeletons chained to the wall.

I slid through the wall and was in a hollow in the masonry with rough steps leading up. It didn't look like a much-traveled way. I followed the route, found an intersecting passage above. It led to another. The walls of the old building were riddled with hideaways, it seemed. I found exits into a dozen rooms, a hidden door into the gardens at the bottom. But none of this was getting me any closer to Renata.

Back on the upper level, I checked out more VIP offices, and in the tenth or twelfth one found my quarry, sitting on the edge of a chair across from a big-shouldered, gray-haired man with career military written all over him. He didn't look pleased.

". . . difficult to explain to the Baron just how it was this subject was able to appear and disappear at will," he was growling. "No one outside Operation Rosebush was aware of the existence of the sub-HQ at the chateau. Yet Bayard was found there; and later, the subject pops up—from nowhere! This is an unacceptable report, Major." He slammed a piece of paper to the desk in front of him and stared at Renata with less than a friendly look.

"My report is factual, Colonel," the little man said. He didn't seem to be much intimidated by the eyebrow treatment. "The fact that I have no hypothesis to offer in explanation doesn't alter my observations."

"Tell me more about the security arrangements you made for holding the subject," the colonel rapped.

"The man is under close guard in a maximum security cell under the chateau," Renata said crisply. "I'll stake my career on that."

"Better not," the colonel said.

Renata shifted in the chair. "Would the colonel care to explain?"

"He's gone. Half an hour after your departure, a routine check showed the cell empty."

"Impossible! I—"

"You're a fool, Renata," the colonel snapped. "The man had already demonstrated that he had unusual resources at his command. Yet you persisted in dealing with him in a routine way."

"I followed service procedures to the letter," Renata came back. Then a thought hit him. "What about Colonel Bayard? He's not . . . ?"

"He's here. I've taken the precaution of cuffing him to his bedstead, and posting two armed guards in the room with him."

"He must be questioned! His conditioning will have to be broken—"

"I'll make that decision, Major! Bayard enjoys a rather special status with top headquarters—"

"Break him, Colonel! He'll confirm what I've told you—and I think he can also offer an explanation of this subject's apparently miraculous powers!"

The colonel picked up a cigar, rolled it between his fingers, then snapped it in two.

"Renata, what the devil is behind this? What's Baron van Roosevelt planning? How does Bayard tie in—and just how much bearing does Richthofen's sudden illness have to do with it?"

"I'm not at liberty to discuss Baron van Roosevelt's plans," Renata said, and returned the colonel's look with interest.

"I'm still your superior officer," the colonel barked. "I demand to know what's going on under my nose!"

"I showed you my report out of courtesy," Renata stood. "I'll make further report to Baron General van Roosevelt, and no one else."

"We'll see about that, Major!" As the colonel jumped to his feet, a red telephone on his desk clanged. He grabbed it up, listened. His expression changed. He looked around the room.

"Right," he said. "I understand."

I moved the shuttle closer, until half of the desk was inside with me, turned up the audio to maximum. Among the crackling and hissing static, I caught the words from the telephone:

"*. . . as though you suspected nothing! It will take us*

another thirty seconds to bring the suppressor into focus . . ."

That was enough for me. I backed off, sent the shuttle out through the side wall, shot through another office where a fat man was kissing a girl, on out through the exterior wall and was hovering over a city park, with hedges, a fountain, winding paths. There was a sharp crackling from the panel, and all my meters jumped at once. The hum of the drive faltered, took on a harsh note. I dropped the shuttle to ground level in a hurry; a power failure in mid-air would be messy. When I tried to head across the park, the shuttle moved six feet and halted with a jolt. The smell of hot wiring was strong now. Flames spouted from behind the panel. I slammed the drive switch off; I was caught but there still might be time to accomplish some denial to the enemy. I switched to full phase, and the color flooded back into the scene on the screen. It took me another five seconds to cycle the door open, jump clear, and thumb the ring switch. The shuttle wavered and faded from view, and dry leaves swirled where it had been a moment before. Then there were white uniforms all around me, closing in with drawn nerve-guns.

7

The building looked different in normal light. My escort walked me along a white-floored hall, up a wide staircase to a big white door flanked by sentries.

Everything in sight was smooth and efficient, but I could feel the tension in the air: a sort of wartime grimness, with lots of hurrying feet in the middle distance. And in the midst of all that spit-and-polish, a curious anomaly caught my eye: a patch of what looked like yellow toadstools, growing in a corner where the marble floor met the wall.

A fellow with a bundle of silver braid looped under his epaulet popped out of the door and we went in. It was a big office with dark-paneled walls and gold-framed paintings of tough-looking old birds in stiff uniform collars, and a desk the size of a bank vault. I looked at the man sitting behind it and met a pair of eyes that literally blazed power.

"Well, Mr. Curlon," he said in a voice like the dirge notes on an organ. "We meet at last."

8

He was a big man, black-haired, with a straight nose and a firm mouth and eyes with a strange, dark shine. He motioned with one finger and the men who had brought me in disappeared. He stood and came around the desk and looked me up and down. He was as tall as I was, which made him over six three, and about the same weight. Under the smooth gray uniform he wore, there was plenty of muscle. Not the draft-horse kind; more like an elegant tyrannosaurus in tailored silk.

"Major Renata made a number of mistakes," he said. "But in the end—you're here, safe and sound. That's all that counts now."

"Who are you?" I asked him.

"I am Baron General van Roosevelt, Chief of Imperial Intelligence—Acting Chief, I should say, during the temporary indisposition of Baron Richthofen." He gave me one of the those from-the-neck-up bows and a smile that was like the sun coming through a black cloud. He clapped me on the shoulder and laughed.

"But between you and myself, Mr. Curlon, formalities are unnecessary." He looked me in the eye, and the smile was gone, but a merry glint still burned there. "I need you, Curlon. And you need me. Between us, we hold the destiny of a world—of many worlds—between our fingers. But I'm being obscure—and I don't mean to be." He waved me to a chair, went to a liquor cabinet and poured two drinks, handed me one, and sat behind the desk.

"Where to begin?" he said. "Suppose I start by assuming that Colonel Bayard has told you nothing—that you have guessed nothing. Listen, then, and I'll tell you of the crisis we face now, you and I . . ."

Chapter Five

"The continuum of multi-ordinal reality is a complex structure, but for purposes of simplicity we can consider it as a bundle of lines stretching from the remote past toward the unimaginable future. Each line is a world, a universe, with its own infinitude of space and stars, separated from its sister worlds by the uncrossable barriers of energy that we know as entropy.

"Uncrossable, that is, until the year 1897, when two Italian scientists, Maxoni and Cocini, stumbled on a principle which changed the course of history—of a billion histories. They created a field in which the energy of normal temporal flow was deflected at what we may consider right angles to the normal direction. Objects and individuals enclosed in the field then moved, not forward in time as in nature, but across the lines of alternate reality. From that beginning grew the Imperium—the government claiming sovereignty over the entire Net of alternate worlds. Your world—which is known to us as Blight Insular Three—is but one of the uncountable parallel universes, each differing only infinitesimally from its neighbor. Like this world, it lies within the vast disaster area we call the Blight, a desert formed when an unfortunate miscarriage in early experimentation with the M-C principle led to the utter destruction of a vast complex of worlds, to the abortion of their destinies into the chaos which you no doubt saw as you crossed that area coming here.

"Among the relationships existing between parallel lines are those linking individuals, Mr. Curlon. Think for a moment: If two worlds differ by only the disposition of two grains of sand on a beach—or of two molecules within a grain of sand—then it follows that analogues of individuals will exist in all those world-lines whose date of common history—the date at which their histories diverged—is later than the birth date of the individual in question. Your case, Mr. Curlon, is an exception—and that fact is at the root of the problem. Your world is an island in the Blight, surrounded not by viable parallel worlds, but by a desert empty of normal life. You are unique, Mr. Curlon—which renders the present situation all the more poignant."

"That's a mild adjective, General," I said. "I'm still listening for what's going to make sinking my boat sound like a friendly move."

"As I said, Major Renata made a number of errors—but his intentions were good. He'd been working here with me, under great strain, for many weeks. As for his mission, consider, Mr. Curlon: You are a man destined for a role in great affairs—yet what did I know of you? Nothing. And time was short. It was necessary—unfortunate, but absolutely necessary—to put you to the test. I apologize for the Major's excessive zeal. Of course, he wasn't aware of the full ramifications of the situation—of your importance to the present contretemps."

"That makes a pair of us."

Roosevelt's expression flickered; there were emotions boiling under that bland façade, but he wasn't the man to show them.

"In the lost worlds of the Blight, your family loomed like a colossus, Mr. Curlon. Now, of all that mighty stock, only you remain." His eyes held me. "The destinies of many men died in the holocaust of the Blight—and human destiny is a force equal to the evolutionary pressure of the Universe itself. Remember: the vast energies choked off by the disaster were not destroyed, but instead shunted into the orgy of patternless vitality that characterizes the Blight. Now those energies seek to reorient themselves, to force a pattern on reality. Unless this power is channeled, guided, given form—our worlds will be engulfed in the cancer of the Blight. Already, signs of the coming plague are here!"

He waved a hand at the gold and blue royal seal on the wall behind him. There were flecks of green on the gilding, and at one corner a tiny crust of mold had formed.

"That crest was polished this morning, Mr. Curlon. And observe this." He pointed to the gold wire insignia on his collar: it was pitted by tarnish. "And this!" he pushed a leather-bound folder across the table. The regal coat of arms embossed on it in silver was bubbly with corrosion.

"Symbols—but symbols that represent the fixed parameters of our cosmos—and those parameters are being eroded, Mr. Curlon!" He leaned back, forced the fire out of his eyes, his voice.

"Unless something is done now, at once, to reinforce the present reality, existence as we know it is doomed, Mr. Curlon."

"All right, General," I said. "I've listened. I don't understand all this, but I've seen enough in the last few hours to keep me from calling you crazy to your face. What is it you want from me? What do you expect me to do about the toadstools growing in the corridors?"

He stood and walked the length of the room, turned and paced back, stopped beside me.

"My plan is a dangerous one; you may think it fantastic, Captain Curlon . . ." I looked the question at him; he nodded and smiled. "I've ordered that you be commissioned in the Imperial Service, and gazetted to my staff," he said casually.

"Thanks, General," I said. "But you can skip the fancies. I'll settle for facts."

He looked disturbed for an instant. "This isn't intended as a bribe," he said, and picked up a thick parchment from the desk. "It's already accomplished—"

"Not without some kind of commitment on my part, it isn't," I said. "Not in any army I ever heard of."

"The oath is required, of course," he said. "A mere formality—"

"A symbol, I believe you said, General. For what it's worth, I'm still a civilian."

"Very well," he tossed the fancy commission aside in a way that I sensed wasn't quite as casual as it looked. "As you wish. Perhaps something Colonel Bayard said has prejudiced you—"

"By the way, where is Bayard now? The last I saw of him he was having a set of stomach cramps brought on by Major Renata's itchy trigger finger."

"Colonel Bayard was misguided. His intentions were good, no doubt, but he was uninformed. I don't wonder that he formed a false impression of the operation on the basis of the few facts he stumbled on."

"I'd like to see him."

"That won't be possible at present; he's in the hospital. However, I contemplate no action against him for breech of discipline, if that's what concerns you. He has an excellent record—until now. He was merely overzealous in this instance."

"You said something about working together. What is it you want from me?"

He stood, came around the desk and clapped me on the shoulder.

"Come along, Captain," he said. "I'll show you."

2

The room he took me to was an underground vault, guarded by three relays of white-jacketed troopers with guns in their hands. One high wall was filled by a ground-glass screen, on which lines and points of light twinkled.

"This is a chart of the Net, covering the area lying within the hundred-thousand-year CH range," Roosevelt said. He picked up a pointer, indicated a red light at the exact center. "This is the Zero-zero world-line of the Imperium.

Here"— he showed me another glowing point, not far away—"is your home-line, B-I Three. Note that all around these isolated lines, for a vast area, there is nothing—a desert. This, Mr. Curlon, is the Blight. Calculations by our physicists tell us that the probability imbalance, dating from the original cataclysm that formed the Blight some seventy years ago, is now seeking equilibrium. Fantastic energies are trapped there in a precarious stasis; energies of the kind that generate reality instant by instant as normal entropy progresses. I needn't tell you of the inconceivable potency of such powers. Consider only that in each instant of time the Universe is destroyed and recreated—and that here, in this blighted region, that process has been aborted, blocked like a choked volcano. For seven decades the pressure has mounted. Now it will no longer be denied. A great probability storm rages at the centroidal point of the Blight. When it blasts through, unless we take some action first, it will carry our world—and all other worlds within a vast range—with it into a limbo of probability disaster which beggars the imagination. Even now, probability waves are moving outward from the holocaust, with results that anyone can see—a mere hint of the holocaust to come."

He grounded the pointer, looked at me long and hard.

"Your destiny is interwoven with that of your world, Mr. Curlon—your fate, your history, are a part of the basic warp of the fabric of the reality we know. We have to seize on that thread—and every other thread we know of, few though they are—and from them, attempt to reweave a viable matrix into which the trapped energies can drain."

I had the feeling he was oversimplifying the problem; but even so, it was too dense for me.

"Keep talking, General," I said. "I'm trying to grope along with you."

"Our lives don't exist in a vacuum, Curlon. We have pasts, roots, antecedents. Actions of men of a thousand years ago affect our lives today, just as our actions of today will repercuss down the ages that come after. Napoleon, Hitler, Caesar, affected their times and all the times to follow. But we stand at a moment where the very texture of existence is strained to the breaking point. What we do, far beyond the ordinary measure of the potency of key individuals, will determine the shape of the world to come. We must act promptly, decisively, correctly. We can afford no weakness, no mistake."

"You're building up to something, General. Why not come to the point."

He pushed a button on a console and the map winked out and another diagram took its place. This one showed an amoeba of pink and red lines twitching and writhing over a grid dotted with glowing points.

"This is a close-range energy chart of the Blight," he said. "Here you see the shifting of the lines of quantum demarcation, as they seek to adjust to the abnormal pressures exerted by the probability storm. In every world-line adjoining the Blight, objective reality is in flux. Objects, people, landscapes, are shifting, changing from moment to moment, day to day. I need not detail for you the pandemonium thus produced. So far we've felt the effects less, here; the Zero-zero line is a stable one firmly rooted in past history by a series of powerful key events. The same is true of your line, B-I Three. For the Blight to engulf these lines would entail the obliteration of basics of human cultural development as powerful as the discovery of fire."

He switched again, this time to a view of a blazing roil like a close-up of the sun.

"This is the center of the probability storm, Mr. Curlon. We've pinpointed its location, in a world-line that was once the seat of a great culture. This is where the key to the crisis will be found. I propose to go there, Mr. Curlon, to find that key."

"It looks as though that would be a lot like jumping down the throat of a live volcano."

"This diagram represents the turmoil of probability energies," Roosevelt said. "On the surface, to an observer within the A-line itself, the storm is not directly apparent. Abnormalities, freaks, impossibilities, the suspension of natural law, the distortion of reality under your very eyes, yes; but the tempest itself rages at a level of energy detectable only to specialized instruments. A man can go there, Mr. Curlon; the dangers he faces will be beyond description—but not perhaps beyond overcoming."

"Once there, then what?"

"Somewhere in that line is a key object, an artifact so inextricably interwoven with the past and future of the line, and of the quantum it controls, that all major probability lines must pass through it, in the way that lines of magnetic force flow through the poles of a magnet. I propose to find and identify that object, and remove it to a safe place."

"Go ahead," I said. "Spell the rest of it out."

"What more is there to say, Mr. Curlon?" Roosevelt gave me the sunny smile again, and his eyes had that dangerous twinkle of a man in love with danger. "I want you with me. I need you—the powers you represent—at my side."

"What makes you think I'll go?"

"I ask you to go—I can't, wouldn't attempt to force you. That would be worse than useless. But remembering the greatness of your line, I believe you'll know where your duty lies."

"Now it's my duty, eh?"

"I think it is, Captain Curlon." He rose and gave me the smile again. This was a man I would have to love or hate; there'd be no middle ground.

"You needn't make your decision now," he said easily. "I've arranged for quarters for you here in my apartments. Get a night's rest; then we'll talk again." His eyes strayed down over my sweater and dungarees, fixed on the knife stuck through my belt.

"I shall have to ask that you leave the, er, weapon with me," he said. "Technically, you're under what is known as RIA—routine interrogational arrest. No point in causing talk."

"I'll keep it," I said. I don't know why. He had an army at his disposal to take it away from me if he felt like it. He leaned forward and frowned at me. His eyes were showing a little controlled anger now.

"Be kind enough to save unpleasantness by placing the knife on my desk," he said.

I shook my head. "It's a sentimental hang-up I have, General. I've carried it so long I'd feel naked without it."

His eyes locked on mine like electronic gun-pointers; then he relaxed and smiled.

"Keep it, then. Now go along and think over what I've said to you. And by tomorrow I hope you've decided to do as I ask."

3

The room they took me to was a little small for a diplomatic reception, but otherwise would have filled the bill OK. After my escort left I poked into a dressing room fit for a Broadway star, a closet that could have slept six with room left over for an all-night poker game, stuck a finger in a bed that looked like an Olympic wrestling mat with tassels. It was fancier than my usual style, but I had an idea I'd be able to sleep on it all right.

I took a shower in a bathroom full of gold faucets and pink marble, and put on the fresh clothes that were laid out for me, after which a waiter in black knee pants and a gold vest arrived with a cart loaded with pheasant on translucent china and wine and paper-thin glasses. While I tucked it away I thought about what I'd learned from Roosevelt. The surface part—the story about parallel worlds and the disaster hanging over them unless he and I did something about it—was all right; as all right as insanity ever is. I didn't understand it, would never understand it—but the evidence was here, all around me. It was the other parts of the general's presentation that bothered me.

Once, when time hung heavy on my hands in a flat-top ready room, I spent some time reading up on games theory. The present situation seemed susceptible to analysis in the light of what I learned then. Roosevelt had tried three gambits: First, when he'd eased the commission at me. Second, when he'd tried to get my agreement to go along with him, in the blind, on a mission into the Blight. And third, when he'd tried to separate me from the knife. I'd resisted all three moves, more by instinct than any logic or plan.

I walked over to the window and looked down at a wall and a cobbled street. The big trees threw shadow patterns over the grass strips and flowerbeds, and the wide sidewalks were full of pretty women and men in bright uniforms with horsetail plumes and buttons that sparked under the lights. Across the park there were shops with bright-lit windows full of plush merchandise, and cafés with open-air terraces and awnings and tables and an odor of fresh-ground coffee and fresh-baked bread. From a bandstand somewhere you could hear an orchestra playing a Straussy sort of waltz—one that had never been heard, back where I came from.

I wondered what Bayard was doing now and what he'd have to say about the latest developments. I'd accepted him at face value, mostly on the basis of the fact that he'd snatched me off my boat just before I started the long swim. But if Roosevelt was telling the truth—if the whole thing had been designed just to test my reactions before pulling me into a key role in world-shaking events . . .

In that case, I should tell Roosevelt all I'd seen at Chateau Gaillard. Maybe there was a clue there for someone who knew how to use it. Or misuse it.

Bayard had known a lot more about the situation than I

did, and he hadn't trusted Renata, or Renata's boss. I wished he could have heard Roosevelt's pitch and given me the other side of the story.

What I needed now was information about Roosevelt, about Bayard, about what was going on and most of all, information about my place in all this—and the meaning of the old piece of steel with the magical property of pointing to other old pieces of steel.

I went to the door and eased it open; there was a guard in a white and gold uniform standing at a rigid parade rest at the far end of the passage. He looked my way and I gave him an offhand wave and he went back to eyes-front. I wasn't exactly under arrest, but they were keeping an eye on me. I started to close the door—and heard a scream like a gutted horse from the room next to mine. The sentry yanked a shiny chrome-plated gun from a polished holster and came on at a run. I took two jumps to the door the yell had come from and jerked at the knob, then stepped back and kicked it open and was looking at a white worm the size of a fire hose looped like a boa constrictor around the crushed body of a man.

4

He was an old man with a purple face and white hair and popped-out eyes and tongue. I was holding the broken sword in my hand; I didn't remember drawing it. It made a sound like an ax hitting a saddle when I brought it down on the worm. It cut through it like cheese, and the severed end whipped around, spattering foul-smelling juices. Something boomed like a cannon behind my ear, and a chunk of worm flew. A ten-foot piece was flapping across the floor and the gun boomed again and it flew up in the air, whipping, while I hacked at another loop that was weaving around on end like a charmed snake. There were four pieces of the thing now and more boiling out through the bathroom door. I heard a gun click on an empty chamber and the guard swore and ended on a gurgling note. I chopped my way through to him, but I was too late. He was wrapped like a mummy and his head was at an angle that meant he'd made his last formation. There were yells from the passage, and the sound of running feet and shots. I cut my way across and into the bathroom. The jade green marble tub was full of worm, writhing up through the drain. I hacked it off, grabbed up a long-handled bath brush and rammed it down the drain, then chopped my way back through the flopping sections and into the hall. What was there was worse than the worm. It looked like a mass of raw meat, bulging up from the stairwell halfway down the corridor. Two men were firing into it, but it didn't seem to mind that much. I came up on it from the side and carved a slice off, and the mass of rubbery stuff recoiled, oozing pink blood. It didn't like cold steel.

"Get knives and swords!" I yelled. "You're wasting time firing slugs in it!"

The mass had bulged along the hall far enough to half cover a door. I burst inward, and I got a glimpse of a woman standing there before it welled through and blocked the opening. I caught just a faint echo of her scream. It took half a dozen good chops to amputate the mass in the door, but I was too late again. All I could see of the girl was a pair of slippered feet sticking out from under the thing like a careless mechanic under a slipped jack.

Back in the hall I saw Roosevelt, in his shirt-sleeves, his teeth bared in what might have been a grin, hewing away at the thing with a two-handed sword. He saw me and yelled, "Curlon, to me!"

Uniformed men were doing what damage they could with ceremonial short-swords, but it was Roosevelt who was driving the thing back. It had bulged in to form a pocket, and he was wading into the pocket, while the rest of the thing bulged alongside, flanking him. I hit it on his left, hacked away a chunk the size of a Shetland pony just as the other side folded in, almost caught him. He stabbed at it, and I cut a swath through and got a stance back to back with him. He seemed to be trying to cut his way to a door that was two-thirds covered and starting to sag. We cleared it, and by then there were a dozen men working on the outer perimeter with swords they'd pulled off walls somewhere. We were ankle-deep in the thin pink blood that drained from every cut we made. I smelled smoke, and saw a pair of firemen in protective suits coming up the stair with oversized blowtorches. The thing flowed away ahead of them, turning black and shriveling. In another minute or two it was all over. I looked at Roosevelt through the smoke and the stink, past him along the corridor that was splashed to the ceiling and reeking like a slaughterhouse.

"Nice," I said, and discovered I was as winded as if I'd just run the four-minute mile. "What was it?"

Roosevelt grinned at me. He was breathing hard, and there was blood on his face, but incredibly, he looked like a man having fun.

"A brisk hour and a quarter," he said. "I congratulate you, Captain. You matched me blow for blow. Not many could have done it." It was a brag, but somehow it didn't sound arrogant. Just truthful.

"You didn't answer the question, General," I said.

His eyes went past me to the foul bulk spread across the blue Oriental carpeting.

"I don't really know," he said. "This was the worst attack so far. The periodicity has decayed to ninety-one hours and the intensity is increasing logarithmically. It doesn't seem to be an animal, in the normal sense of the word—merely a mass of flesh, growing wild."

"What kind of flesh?" I growled. It made my skin crawl to look at it.

His eyes met mine. "Human flesh, Mr. Curlon," he said.

I nodded. "I'm still not sure about all this, General; but if this is what you're fighting, I'm with you."

He gave me the smile, reached out and caught my hand with a grip like a rock-crusher.

"With you behind me—"

"Beside you," I cut in.

He nodded, still smiling. "Beside me, then. Perhaps we can yet prevail."

5

I didn't get much sleep for the next couple of nights. When I wasn't busy bone-bending with an unarmed combat master named Lind, I was listening to lectures on field operation, and doing my napping with a hypnotaper strapped to my skull, pumping me full of background data on the history of the Blight.

There were a few other trainees around. One was a beautiful Oriental-looking girl from an A-line where the Chinese had settled America back in the ninth century, and had met the Romans head-on along the Mississippi in 1776. She was headed for a place where a horde of backward, matriarchal Mongols were getting ready to sweep across a feudal Europe. It seemed that she fitted the bill of particulars for the incarnation of the goddess Chiu-Ki, a sort of celestial Dragon Lady. And a big coal-black man with a fierce look—maybe because of the stainless steel peg through his nose—had been recruited from a Zulu-ruled African empire to help organize a grass-roots resistance to a murder-suicide cult that was decimating the enslaved blacks in a line where the Greeks had developed science in the pre-Christian era and used it to conquer the known world before stagnation set in. I met one fellow who was a classic example of the Australian Bushman—but in his line his tribe had made it big on the mainland. He had a hard time not wrinkling his flat nose at the strange odors, but he was a gentleman. He treated us like equals.

During the week, I tried several times to see Bayard, but Roosevelt always put me off. The colonel was a sick man, he said. Pneumonia had set in, as it often did after a taste of the neurac. He was in an oxygen tent, and no visitors allowed.

Then the day came when the general came down and watched for half an hour while Lind tried to throw me on my ear; but I got lucky and threw him instead.

"You're ready," Roosevelt said. "We'll leave at midnight."

6

The shuttle terminus was a huge bright-lit room with a polished white floor marked off in orange lines, with shuttles ranked between the lines. There were little one-man scouts and big twenty-man passenger transports, some bare, functional boxes, some fancy VIP jobs, some armored, some fitted up to look like moving vans or delivery trucks. There was a steady, high-pitched whine, and a constant booming and buffeting from air displacement as shuttles came and went. I'd never seen any of it before, but it was all familiar from the sessions under the hypnotaper.

Technicians in white coveralls worked over machines, standing at little desks that were spaced along the aisles. Across the room I saw a party of men in costumes like Spanish conquistadores, and another group in Puritan black.

"Protective coloration," Roosevelt said. "Our agents always try to blend with the background. In our case, no disguises are necessary. As far as I know, there's no human life left where we're going."

The technicians fitted us into our suits—old-fashioned flyers' outfits with lightweight diving helmets. They checked us over with a minumum of formality, and we strapped in and closed the hatch. Roosevelt looked sideways at me and gave me the thumbs-up sign. "Ready?"

"It's your show, General," I said. He nodded and threw in the drive control. The whining hum started up; the light outside faded. The walls and roof quivered and disappeared, and we were perched two feet above a vacant lot full of weeds and blown dust under the open sky.

Chapter Six

We didn't talk much, crossing the Blight, following the *beep-beep*! of the tracer turned to our target. I watched the blasted landscape flow past while Roosevelt monitored fifty dial faces at once and corrected the control settings from time to time for no reason I could make out. For a while we skimmed above a plain of shattered rock, where smoke boiled up from fumaroles and volcanic cones that threw a red glow across the sky. Then there was an ocean of oily, scummed fluid that broke in sluggish foamy waves. And then land again: cinder-black, with pale flames licking over it until it coalesced into a sea of lava, dull-red and bubble-pocked. All the while, the clouds over the moon never moved.

The lava darkened, hardened, turned to a dusty plain. Green appeared, and strange, scabbed trees shot up in clumps of two or three. Vines spread, and ruins poked up among them. A slab of rock came into view, tilted up by the roots of a fifty-foot dandelion with hooks all along the stem. "We're close," Roosevelt said. "That's the highway leading into the city of Fontrevrault."

He corrected course to bring us in over the old road leading off through the nightmare jungle, between fallen walls and rusted steel frameworks that were trellises now for ropes of flesh entwined with warty vines with leaves like rotted canvas curving over clusters of oversized, blind rodent-heads like bunches of fruit. They had no eyes, but there were plenty of teeth showing, set in the husks of the plants that nourished them.

The forest opened out, thinned. Tall ochre and rust

buildings loomed up on both sides, like jungle temples in Yucatan. Fungus grew on the granite and marble, and the bronze statues of gods and goddesses were overgrown with cancerous-looking corrosion. The forest retreated to expose a paved plaza, and a mountain of marble chips and tiles and glass behind a set of hundred-foot columns tangled in vines.

Some of the discolored blotches faded from the marble; the wide sweep of the plaza smoothed minutely. A fountain at the center that had been scattered slid back into shape, all but the head of the mermaid at the center. Then there was a sharp *be-beep*! and the amber light went on on the panel. We had arrived in the eye of the probability storm.

2

Roosevelt slung an instrument pack over his shoulder and checked the dials on it.

"You and I will be the first men ever knowingly to set foot in the Blight," he said. "And if we do anything wrong—make the slightest error—we'll be the last. One mistake here could send our entire cosmos tumbling."

"Fair enough," I said. "Just one question: How do we know what might be a mistake?"

"Follow your instinct, Mr. Curlon," Roosevelt said and gave me a smile that seemed to be loaded with obscure significance. Then he opened up and we stepped out into a nightmare fantasy.

All around, tall buildings reared up against a sky of broken clouds over a yellow moon. The nearest was made of polished crimson stone, carved into patterns where huge vines clung, casting black shadows. From it, white marble steps led down to a walk lined with giant oaks on which green orchids grew. Vivid-colored birds sang in branches that arched across the tiled avenue. And behind this island of comparative order, the jungle loomed like a besieging army.

"Amazing," Roosevelt said in a low voice. "It's almost intact, Curlon—almost as it was in the days of its glory! There is the Summer Palace—and there the Cathedral—and the Académie des Artes—still standing, in the midst of carnage!"

"Hard to believe we're in the center of a storm," I said. "It's as peaceful as a graveyard."

"A mighty empire died here," Roosevelt said. "Where we stand, triumphal armies marched, with kings at their heads. The fairest women in any universe rode their carriages along these avenues. Here art and culture rose to their highest peak—to be dashed to the lowest depths. Grieve for it, Curlon; for magnificence, lost forever."

"For now I'll settle for finding what we came for."

"Quite right," Roosevelt said in a suddenly brisk tone. He checked the dials strapped to his wrist, then tilted back his helmet.

"The air is all right," he said. I tried it. It was hot, steamy, like a greenhouse at night. There was a steady surf-roar of sound: the rustle and scrape of leaves, the rasp and creak of stems bending in the breeze, the cluck and groan and hiss and whine and bleat of animal voices, as if we were in the middle of the world's biggest zoo, and all the inmates were having bad dreams. The tiled pavement under our feet was chipped and shattered, but navigable. Lichenous vines as big as your wrist snaked across it, and the moonlight glinted on spines like poniards that bristled along them.

"To protect the shuttle, I'm putting it on an oscillatory circuit that will prevent it from phasing into identity with any A-line," Roosevelt said. "When we're ready to leave, I can recall it with a remote signaler."

I watched as it winked out of sight with a boom of imploding air. As we started off, something moved among the greenery; a thing like a hairy snake dragged its length over a fallen tree-trunk, gaping a dog's head at us. At first I thought there were no legs, but then I saw them—dozens of them, all sizes, growing out of the ten-foot body at random angles. A vine hissed and struck at it, and the jaws snapped and another ten feet of body flopped into view, with more heads, all biting at once. The vine took a few more loops around the wormlike body and squeezed. Somewhere a cat yowled, and underbrush crashed and the yowl became a scream.

"Don't use your gun except in extremity," Roosevelt warned. "To take life here—any life—is to interfere with the probability equation. Even the slightest realignment could interfere with the shuttle recall signal."

There was an archway across the avenue ahead almost lost under its load of washtub-sized toadstools, but across the top carved figures and flowers were still visible. Roosevelt consulted his dials again.

"Our destination appears to be the Royal Archives," he said. "It's just ahead."

The side street faced a wall of foliage that had been a park. On our side, there was a monumental façade, festooned with ragged vines. Some of the windows still had glass in them, but most of them were blind, like eyes afflicted with green cataracts. Where the door had been, there was a gap in the screen of vines.

"Something's been using that entrance," I said. "Something the size of a rhinoceros."

"Still—that's where we must go," Roosevelt said, and pushed through a screen of limp, yellow-spotted leaves the size of garrison flags. There was a path through the mat of moss on the floor, where tiles showed. We followed it fifty feet to a dead end. Roosevelt unshipped a handlight and played it over a wall of impacted vines.

"We'll have to cut through." He changed the torch setting, and the beam dimmed to deep red, sliced through the tangled growth. In half a minute he had cut a hole big enough to climb through.

He clipped the torch to his belt and went ahead. I started after him, and heard a rumble like a Bengal tiger disturbed at his nap. I came through fast, grabbing for my gun, and saw moonlight on low walls, black lawn, a fountain with water. Roosevelt was backed against the carved Neptune, facing something right out of the fairy-tale books. It had a long, feline body, a maned neck, a beak like an eagle—if eagles had beaks two feet long. The legs were scaled from the midpoint down and ended in talons like the big claw in a wrecking yard. It was a griffin, half lion and half eagle, and both halves were closing in for the kill.

3

I yelled and fired high to distract the thing. It reared up and danced around on its hind legs to face me, showing an expanse of snow-white underbody and giving me a good look down the red throat behind the beak. The eyes were the size of Dixie cups, three concentric circles around yellow irises. The outer circle was scales—iridescent silver ones. Darker scales ran back across the face and ended where the white mane began. A pointed black tongue licked out like a snake between the halves of the knife-edged beak. I saw all this in a couple of fast seconds while I backed away and wondered just what Roosevelt would call an extremity.

"Hold your fire!" he called. "It's tame!" I started to ask him what his idea of wild was, when I saw what he meant. There was a harness strapped around the thing's chest, almost hidden under the mane. Silver ornaments dangled from the black leather, jingled as it moved. It dropped down to all fours less than ten feet from me, gave a scream that ended in a yowl, and sat down on its haunches. Its timing was good; in another half second I'd have blown its chest open. Which would have been a serious mistake, because just then the owner came walking out of the shadows.

Chapter Seven

I'd gaped pretty hard at the snake-dog, and the griffin had held my attention, too; but neither of them was anything at all to what I saw now.

It was a girl: tall, high-bosomed, long-legged, with skin as white as the fallen marble columns, and dark copper hair piled up high over a face that was like the one you dream about, that smiles and is lost forever, and you wake up sick with yearning. She was dressed in a flimsy swath of white gauzy stuff that clung to her hips and thighs like wet tissue paper and floated when she moved. She came straight up to the thing that had me cornered and said, "Aroint thee, Vrodelix! An ill greeting for visitors!" It dropped its head and whined like an overgrown puppy.

The girl pushed the monster aside and looked at me. Her eyes were dark blue, and they glistened in the moonlight. I knew those eyes; I'd seen them in the dream.

"Are you a man?" she said. "Or a god?" Her tone indicated that both choices were equally likely. I told her and she nodded.

"I'm glad. I am a mortal woman." She looked across at Roosevelt, who had come up to us. He gave her a courtly bow and the smile.

"But *you* are a god," she said.

"Only a man, my dear," he said. "Pieter Roosevelt, at your service—and this is Richard Curlon."

She smiled up at him, and I felt a strange feeling that somehow I'd missed out on something rare and valuable.

"And I am Ironel, Pieter," she said.

"You live here alone?" Roosevelt was asking.

"Oh, no. Vrodelix is with me." She ran a hand along the sleek, curved neck of the nightmare animal. "And I have other friends—and now, two new ones!" She caught Roosevelt's hand and then mine and smiled from one to the other of us, and we grinned back.

"Tell me about your other, ah, friends, Ironel," Roosevelt said in the gentle, fatherly tone he had adopted with her.

"Of course, Pieter! There is Ronizpel the Climber, and Chazz the Dweller Below, and Arnq of the Spines—and many more!"

"All animals?"

She had to think that one over. "Mostly," she said. "Except for Chazz—I think. But you'll meet them soon. Oh, how glad they'll be you've come!" She stopped, as if she had just remembered something. "But Old Garff—I'm not sure *he*'ll be pleased."

"How long have you lived here?" Roosevelt wanted to know.

"Why—forever." She sounded surprised at the silly question.

"Where are your parents?"

"What are parents?"

"The people who raised you—taught you to speak, to dress yourself so prettily?"

"Why . . . 'tis a novel thought, Pieter! Must one *learn* to talk as I taught Arnq to weave his nets o'er the Dark Places?" She touched the soft fold of the cloth she wore. "As for my garment—'tis made for me by Arnq, of course." She looked at Roosevelt's nylon suit, touched my sleeve. "I must show him your weaver's work; 'twill set him a task, to make stuff like it." She laughed, pleased by the idea.

"Are there no other people here—like you, and us?" Roosevelt persisted.

"But—we are not like!" Ironel laughed. "You are taller

than I, and your hair is short, and your shoulders wide and your chest flat—not like me." She touched her body, ran her hand down her slim waist as if to sense the differences with her fingertips.

"We're men," Roosevelt said, smiling faintly. "You're a woman. Are there other humans of either sex here?"

That seemed to puzzle her. "No, none," she said.

"What do you eat? How do you keep warm in winter?"

"Why—Chazz brings me roots from the deep earth, and Ronizpel knows where the grapes and melons ripen soonest. And when the whiteness falls, I dwell indoors, and Arnq swathes the windows with his finest weaving to hold back the cold."

Vrodelix whined, and while the girl was soothing him, Roosevelt stepped close to me.

"Are we to believe this poor natural maid lives all alone here as she says? Is it possible?"

"It looks that way. For some reason the Blight seems to stay clear of this little patch of ground. You said it was the eye of the storm. The eye of a hurricane is a dead calm."

Ironel was back beside us, smiling. "Come," she said. "Now I'll show thee my playthings!" She towed us across a flagstone walk between tended flowerbeds where black and gold fungus blossoms grew between roses and daisies. We went through an archway and across a tiled hall and up stairs into a wide, shadowy corridor that was blocked twenty feet away by fallen masonry; but the part that was clear was swept clean. She opened a door on a room with a deep black carpet and high, glassless windows with curtains of the same gauzy stuff as her clothing. There was a high bed with a white silk canopy over it, decorated with a floral design in gold thread. She knelt by a big chest with a carved lid and opened it and lifted out a bolt of scarlet cloth.

"Is it not pretty?" she said and stretched a length of it across her body. I had to agree it was pretty.

She took out a smaller box and poured gold coins out on

the rug. I knelt to gather them up and discovered that the rug was a layer of moss, as smooth and even as black velvet.

"And these!" she dumped jewels among the coins; they sparkled like hot embers.

"And these are my dearest treasures!" she said, and spilled colored seashells out among them.

She laughed. "And now we must sort them, and put them away. Is it not a fine game?"

Roosevelt picked up a big square-cut ruby with an incised crest.

"Where did you get this?" his voice grated roughly. His eyes bored into hers. She didn't seem to notice the change of pace.

"In the Pretty Place," she said. "There are many more, but I liked these the best."

"Show me!" he snapped.

"Easy, General," I said. "We play the young lady's game first, then yours."

For a moment his eyes clashed with mine; then he relaxed, smiled, laughed aloud. He got down on his knees and started picking up seashells and placing them in a careful heap.

2

She led us down into a wide, moonlit avenue, almost roofed over by vines. Vrodelix paced beside her, making hissing sounds and acting increasingly nervous as we came closer to the fallen buildings at the far end.

"Poor beast, he remembers the Thing-with-eight-legs and the Fanged Ones," Ironel said. "They frightened him, ere he slew them."

She pointed to a tall, mold-blackened building nestled up against the barricade of rubble. "Vrodelix mislikes me to go there—but with you by me, naught can emperil us."

"The State Museum," Roosevelt said. He looked at the

instrument strapped to the underside of his wrist, but if it told him anything he didn't say so.

We went through a weed-choked entrance, crossed a hall that was carpeted and walled with vines, went up a wide, curved staircase. The second floor was in better condition. There were glass-topped cases here, dusty but intact. Old paintings hung on the walls, mold-spotted faces in strange ruffs and plumed helmets peering down from leafy shadows, but their stiff expressions looked more frightened than arrogant. We went on into the next room, where formerly elaborate uniforms with knee-boots and capes with moth-eaten tiger-skin facings hung on decaying dummies with vacant, horrified faces. Fancy saddles and tattered regimental flags were displayed along with lances and dueling pistols and hand-tooled matchlocks, all draped with spiderwebs.

"Now—you must close your eyes," Ironel said, and took our hands. Her fingers were slim and cool and soft. She watched to make sure I followed instructions, then led the way up three steps, and across more floor, around obstructions, then down again. I was just beginning to wonder how long the blindman's buff went on when she stopped and said, "Open your eyes!"

Colored moonlight streamed down through a stained-glass window on a gray stone floor leading away to an altar with slim columns and a gold canopy and silver candlesticks. A silver-mounted reliquary box lay there. There was a stone sarcophagus before the altar, with the carved figure of a Crusader on it, dressed in full armor, his hands crossed over the hilt of his sword that lay on his chest like a crucifix.

"Dost like my Pretty Place?" Ironel asked in a breathless voice.

"We like it very much indeed," Roosevelt said softly. "Will you show me where you found the signet stone?"

"Here." Ironel turned to a brass-bound coffer sitting on wooden trestles to the left. Roosevelt lifted the lid. The soft light winked on rings and armlets and brooches—a magpie's trove of trinkets. Ironel lifted a chain of soft gold links and held it against her, then dropped it and took a tiny silver chain with a dangling amethyst.

"This is prettier," she said. "Do thee not think so, Pieter?"

"Much prettier, my dear." His eyes moved past her, roving over the details of the little chapel, back to the dial on his wrist. He started toward the altar, and Ironel made a distressed sound and caught at his hand.

"Pieter—no! Thou must approach no closer!"

He gave her a smile that was more grim than comforting. "It's all right," he said in a soothing tone. "I mean only to have a look at it." He brushed her hand away.

"Pieter—you mustn't! Bad things will happen if we intrude there! Canst thou not feel it in the very air?"

He wasn't listening. He took another step—and stopped. Far away, something rumbled. The floor trembled, and a piece of glass cracked in the window. I stepped to his side.

"You're a guest here," I said. "Maybe you'd better play house rules."

He shot me a look like a harpoon. "I'll decide that," he said, and started on.

I caught his arm. It was like grabbing an oak rail. He strained to pull free and I strained to hold him back. Neither of us seemed to be gaining.

"The girl says 'no,' General," I said. "Maybe she has a reason."

"Come to your senses, Curlon," he said, still sounding calm. "Remember what we came here to find!"

"You said yourself the equation is in delicate balance," I said. "Take it slowly, until you know what you're doing."

There was another rumble, closer this time. I felt the floor move under my feet. The griffin raked his talons on the floor and yowled. Ironel whimpered; I heard a sound from above, looked up in time to see a safe-sized stone dropping at me. I dived to the side; the smash was like switch-engines colliding. Rock chips flew like shrapnel. Roosevelt whirled and ran for the altar. The griffin hissed and reared to strike at him, but Ironel shrieked and the animal crouched back, his ears flat and Roosevelt ran past him. I started after him and a marble pilaster crashed down between us. The floor was heaving like jelly, with broken stone and fragments of ceiling mosaic and stained glass and ironwork and chunks of statuary dancing on it like water drops in a hot skillet. Roosevelt ran into the thick of it; stones fell around him like bomb fragments. A small one hit him on the shoulder, but he stayed on his feet, staggering now but still trying to reach the altar. He was six feet from it when the canopy over it sagged and went down. One of the columns fell. It barely brushed him, but it threw him ten feet. He skidded in the dust and lay still, a broken doll. The rumble died away. A few stray pebbles clattered down into silence.

Ironel went to her knees beside Roosevelt. She touched his face. "Is he dead?" she whispered.

I checked him over. There was a nasty dent in his skull. His breathing was shallow and rasping, but his pulse was solid.

"He's badly hurt," I said. "But not dead—yet."

With Ironel's help I got him on my back, carried him back to her sleeping room, and laid him out on the bed in the dark.

Chapter Eight

Daylight came after a long time. Ironel was asleep, her head on Roosevelt's bed. When I woke her, she smiled at me.

"He still lives, Richard," she said. I checked his pulse again. It was still there, but his breathing was shallow and ragged. I touched the depressed fracture over his eye.

"I've got to do something about this," I said. "Do you have any way to make fire?"

"Ronizpel fears the fire," she said. "But he will bring it to me."

I examined the wound. There was one main bone splinter, with some smaller fragments. Ironel came back with a shallow brass tray with glowing embers in it. I didn't ask questions, just added some wood to the coals and got a brisk fire going, and sterilized my knife blade in it.

I made an incision across the wound, crossed it with another, and folded back the flaps of skin. Ironel stepped in like a trained nurse, following every step, acting without even words from me. While she held the incision open, I used a hook bent from wire and heat-sterilized to lift the big splinter back into position, then probed for the others. After a while I was finished. I closed the wound and he was still breathing. Ironel used red silk thread to stitch up the cuts. She finished and then sat beside him, watching his face. I found a corner and went to sleep.

2

I woke up with light in my face; Ironel was beside me; her face was cameo-pale against the shadows.

"Richard—I am afraid for Pieter."

I got up and went to him. He lay on his back on the bed. His eyes were closed and sunken, his face drawn into a tortured rictus. He snarled between his locked teeth, and his hands raked at the coverlet.

"No," he ground out the words. "Never . . . bend the knee . . . better . . . eternal destruction . . ." his voice ran off into a mutter.

I put my fingers against his neck. He was hot as new-cast iron. The wound in his forehead was swollen and inflamed.

"I'm sorry," I said. "We need medicines we don't have."

"Richard," the girl said. "Chazz says we must bring Pieter to him."

I looked at her. Her eyes were big and dark, her hair red-black, a damp curl against her white skin.

"We shouldn't move him."

"But—Chazz cannot come here, Richard!"

I looked at Roosevelt. I didn't know much about medicine, but I'd seen a dying man before. I lifted him and the girl led the way down through the dark halls among the black vines and the fallen statuary and out into the perfumed night.

3

Stone mermaids cavorted in a dry fountain at the center of a weed-choked garden. Ironel pulled aside the leafy branch of a twisted bush that grew up through a crack in the basin, exposing an opening. Stone steps led down at a steep angle into an odor of mushrooms and wet clay. Ironel led the way. In a room at the bottom, she flashed my handlight on sagging shelves loaded with dusty wine bottles. At the far side the wall was broken away by what looked like a giant rat-hole. The odor that came from it was like the ape-house at the zoo.

Ironel didn't seem to notice. She went to the opening, called:

"Chazz—it's I, Ironel—and Richard, my friend. We've brought Pieter!"

A sound came back, like boulders grinding together under the earth. Ironel turned to me.

"Chazz says we may bring him in."

I went down through the opening; it was a smooth-walled tunnel cut through damp earth. It curved, dipped, ended at a complicated wall of lumpy wet leather that blocked the tunnel. Ironel put the light on the wall and I saw it was a face, six feet high, six feet wide, with a vast hooked nose, sunken eyelids that lifted to show the glint of eyes the size of basketballs. There was matted hair as coarse as mammoth fur on the cheeks and on the sloping, wrinkled forehead. Where there wasn't hair, the skin was black, scaled, and creased like a rhino's hide. The edges of broken teeth the size of bargain tombstones showed under the purple edge of the lip. The mouth opened and the voice rumbled forth.

"He says to put him down here," Ironel relayed. I did as she asked. Roosevelt lay like a corpse, death-pale now. The big eyes roved over him. A tongue like a pink feather blanket peered out from the vast mouth, tested the air, went in again.

"This one made the rocks fall," the big voice boomed out, clearer now—or maybe I was just getting used to hearing an earthquake talk.

"He didn't know, Chazz dear," Ironel said in a pleading tone. "He meant no harm."

"A stone hurt me," Chazz said. He rotated his huge skull, and the edge of a black-crusted cut big enough to lay an arm in came into view.

"Poor Chazz—did it hurt very much?"

"Not much, Ironel." The face came back up and a tear that would have filled a teacup splashed down across the leather face. "Don't feel bad for Chazz. Chazz is all right, Ironel."

"And—can you help Pieter?"

Again 'n incredible eyeballs rotated, stared at the unconscious man. The lids came down, half-covering them like wrinkled leather blinds.

"I can try," the monster rumbled. "I feel the hurt place ... there. Bad, bad hurt—but it's not that which is killing Pieter. No—it's the things that pull—there and there! But I push ... push against them ..." his voice went into a mutter like a glacier breaking apart in a spring thaw. Roosevelt stirred, made vague sounds. Ironel put her hand on his forehead. I held the light and saw the color come slowly back into his face. He sighed and his hands moved restlessly, then lay still. His breathing eased.

"Ahhh," Chazz groaned. "Bad things still there, Ironel! I fix him—but I feel bad things stir there still! Better I kill him now—"

"Chazz—no!" Ironel threw herself half across Roosevelt. "You mustn't!"

"I feel things there, inside him," Chazz said. "Things that make me afraid!"

"He's only a man, Chazz—he said so himself. Like Richard! Tell him, Richard!" Ironel caught at my arm. "Tell Chazz that Pieter is our friend!"

"What kind of bad things do you feel inside him, Chazz?" I asked the big face. He rolled his whale's eyes at me.

"When the stones fell, I felt them," he said. "And when I reached into him—I felt them again. Black things prowl there, in the red caverns of his sleeping brain, Richard. He would mold all the world to an image he keeps secret there."

"Back home, he's an important man," I said. "He came here to try to save his world. He made a mistake, and it almost killed him. I don't think there's any harm in him now."

Chazz groaned. "I have known him in my dreams, as I slept here under the earth. Why does he come, Richard? And why you? For of you, too, I have dreamed, moving

81

across the bright, restless pattern of the world. A doom hangs about your head, and about his. But I cannot tell which doom is the stronger." He groaned again. "I fear him, Richard. But for Ironel's sake, I give him his destiny. Now take him from me. His mind stirs and the pain of that stirring cuts to my heart."

I lifted Roosevelt and carried him back through the stinking tunnel and up to Ironel's room.

4

She woke me with half a golden melon on a gold plate and a cluster of red grapes the size of plums. Roosevelt was better, now, she said. I went over and looked at him, lying there on his back, still unconscious. He didn't look any different to me, but his temperature seemed to be normal, and his pulse and breathing too. Maybe I was a better brain surgeon than I thought.

Ironel took me for a tour of her kingdom: the lower floors of the building where she slept, the garden, what was left of the street the earthquake had shaken up. With the early morning light slanting down through the leaves that overgrew it, it had a sort of eerie, silent beauty. Ironel led me by the hand, showed me little clumps of flowers growing in hidden places, a clear pool in a basin that must have been a beautiful fountain once, led me to where there were pretty stones lying scattered in the rank grass—the fragments of an alabaster statue.

We went down chipped marble steps under huge old trees and bathed in a black pool, climbed up in a ruined tower, and looked out through a stone-filigreed window at the view of other towers thrusting up through the jungle. In the evening, we sat on a bench in the garden and listened to the hooting and screeching and hissing of night things that prowled just beyond the borders of the garden. Sometimes she talked, chattered away about her friends and her games; other times she sang strange little tuneless songs.

And sometimes, she just smiled into the vague distance, like a flower, glad to be alive. There were a lot of questions I wanted to ask, but I didn't ask them. She was like a sleeping child; I didn't want to wake her. That night she came to my bed and slept with me, like a child.

The second day passed, and Roosevelt woke up, gave us a faint smile, and went back to sleep. The next day he stayed awake. He seemed to be his old self, assurance and all—except for the hollow-cheeked look. He professed to have no recollection of anything from the time we'd met the girl.

He mended fast then. On the fourth day, he was up and walking. On the fifth day, on my way back from an expedition to the edge of the jungle to gather fruit, I heard an angry yowl from the direction of the park, followed by shots. I knew that yowl—it was Vrodelix, and he was mad. I dropped the red and yellow mangoes I had collected and ran for the gates. Ten feet inside the park, I found the griffin, stretched beside the dolphin fountain, with three holes in him. He moaned and tried to get up, and fell back, dead, his beak gaping. I ran on across the park, up the steps. I shouted for Ironel, but there was no answer. Something made a soft sound behind me, and I turned to see Roosevelt come out of shadows with his nerve-gun aimed at my head.

"I'm sorry, Curlon," he said. "But there's no other way." He pulled the trigger and the world blew up in my face.

5

I was lying on my back, dreaming that Roosevelt was bending over me. His face was thin, hollow-cheeked, and the wound over his eye stood out like a big X marked in lipstick. His voice came from someplace as far away as the stars, but the words were clear enough.

"Get on your feet, Curlon. I've paralyzed your volitional

centers, but you can hear me. We have a duty to perform."

I felt myself climbing to my feet. They seemed to be miles below my head, which floated all alone in a rarified level high above the clouds that drifted just at the edge of vision. My hands were wired together in front of me.

"That way," Roosevelt said. We went out across the garden, past the gentle, dead monster lying on the flagstones, into the ruined street. There was a high, humming noise inside my head, and the light was strange, as though there were an eclipse in progress. We entered the museum, went up the stairs littered with plaster and fragments of a skylight, into the big hall where the armored mannikins lay strewn around like disaster victims. In the chapel, the sun came through the broken window like a spotlight. The altar was still standing, with the ruins of the golden canopy around it. There was a feeling in the air as if the whole world was a bowstring, stretched to the breaking point.

"Go ahead of me," Roosevelt ordered. I picked my way through the rubble, stepped over the broken sarcophagus, brushed away the rotted strands of a velvet cape, stopped in front of the altar.

"Take the box," Roosevelt ordered. I picked it up awkwardly in my wired hands. It was heavy, and the surface tingled as though an electric current were running through it. I felt the current in my feet, too. The floor vibrated under me. There was a rumbling sound, like distant thunder. Roosevelt's face was strained in a tight, baredteeth look that wasn't a smile.

"Give it to me," he said. I handed it over as the rumble grew louder.

"Lo, the very heavens attend our enterprise," he said, sounding as though he meant it. "But we have what we want. Now we'll go."

He turned away and I followed. A section of carved stone toppled from up high, smashed down a few feet away from us. Other things fell, but none of them touched us. As we reached the door, the roof came down behind us. On the stair, I felt the stones breaking up under my feet, but they held until we were down in the big hall; then they came tumbling down.

Outside, the street was a sea of heaving rubble. The building across the way sagged and leaned and fell into the plaza.

We jumped across broken pavement slabs that tilted and ground together like an ice floe breaking up. A tree fell, trailing a snarl of vines, and back in the jungle something as massive as an apartment house loomed up, bellowing.

"The centroid of the probability storm is moving, following us," Roosevelt called to me. "It's success, Curlon—if we can reach the shuttle before this enclave of antiprobability collapses! Stay close to me!" He ran, and I ran with him, while the world came apart around us.

6

In the clearing where we'd left the shuttle on half-phase, Roosevelt took the signaler from the pouch clipped to his belt. I saw something moving in the trees just above him, but I made no effort to say anything. It eased out from under a spray of tent-sized leaves, a spider with a body as big as a bathtub, thick, bristly legs, faceted eyes the size of dinner plates. It swung out on a clotted, grayish cord, a pair of pinchers at its fore end cocked and ready.

"No, Ronizpel!" Ironel's voice cried out behind us, and the spider-thing checked just long enough for Roosevelt to draw his gun and fire a burst of mini-slugs into the swollen abdomen ten feet above him. It burst, and purple-black fluid spewed down. The thing fell, thrashing its eight legs, and Ironel screamed and rushed to it while Roosevelt pumped more rounds into the dying thing. He jumped past her, knocking her aside, pressed the recall button of the signaler. I felt the buzzing in the air around me, saw the light darken, taking on a tarnished tinge like the light before a thunderstorm. A gust of air whirled leaves up, and the shuttle phased into identity, low, black, deadly-looking. Its door slid open to spill white light out into the gloom.

"Curlon—get in!" Roosevelt shouted. The ground shook under me as I walked past the weeping girl and the gutted spider. To my left, the jungle crashed and burst open and the ground rose up and split and the head of Chazz rose up into view, squinting against the light. His eyes went to the girl, and his mouth opened in a howl of rage. Roosevelt brought the gun up and fired into the big face, and chunks of flesh flew and black blood welled out of the craters, and Chazz bellowed in agony; then I was inside, and Roosevelt was behind me, slamming the hatch. He produced handcuffs, chained me to the contoured seat. The screen glowed pink, then cleared to a view of the outside. Chazz had forced his shoulders up through the earth, and his hands, huge and gnarled with chipped black nails as big as coal scuttles, groped out toward the girl. He touched her with one finger, and then the giant head slumped, and Roosevelt threw the drive switch in and the scene flowed like wax in the sun, as the jungle closed in over the spot where Ironel's garden had been.

Chapter Nine

I came up out of a drugged sleep to see early morning sunshine glowing through curtains at an open window. I had a headache like a cracked anvil. Roosevelt was sitting in a brocaded chair beside the bed, dressed in a fantastic outfit that somehow, on him, looked natural enough: a short, loose coat with a fur collar, tight breeches, slippers with jeweled pompons, a big gold chain across his chest, and jewels everywhere, stitched to his sleeves, sparkling in finger rings.

He said "Good morning" in a cheery tone and passed me a cup of coffee. "We've been through a difficult time," he went on. "But it's over now, Curlon. I regret the necessity for the things I was forced to do—but I had no choice. And we succeeded, you and I. Now the victory and all its fruits are ours." He said this in a low voice, but his black eyes glowed like a man looking at visions.

I tried the coffee. It was hot and strong, but it didn't help my head any.

"You understand, don't you?" His eyes probed mine. "A great new destiny is taking shape—for you as well as me. Think of it, Curlon! Who hasn't wished to seize the sorry scheme of things entire, and mold it nearer to his heart's desire? Well—we've done it—together! Out of the ashes of the old, a new world rises—a world in which our fates loom like colossi over the faceless mob! The world that should have been, Curlon, a world of might and glory, such as has never before been seen—spread at our feet like a carpet! We've turned back the clock of fate, set history back on a course that seemed doomed forever!"

"What about the girl?" I asked.

"I'm sorry; she was a shadow in a twilight world. And you, I'm afraid, were caught up in her spell. I did what I had to do. I would have brought her with us, but it was impossible. The fabric I'm weaving is too fragile at this stage to support the transfer of a key figure from a peripheral A-line."

"I don't know what you're doing, Roosevelt," I said. "But whatever it is, the price is too high."

"One day you'll understand, Curlon. Of all mankind you'll understand best. Because, out of all the millions of pawns on the board, you alone are my compeer; like mine, your destiny is entwined with that of the new world that's taking shape."

"Count me out, General," I said. "I want no part of your operations. If you'll tell me where my pants are, I'll be going now."

Roosevelt shook his head, smiling a little. "Curlon, don't talk like a fool. Do you have any idea where you are?"

I got out of the bed, shakily, and went to the window and looked down on lawns and flowerbeds that were almost familiar.

"This is a world-line far removed from the turmoil of the Blight," Roosevelt said as I dressed in the loose shirt and tight pants laid out for me. "Its common-history date with your world is 1199 A.D. We're in the city of Londres, capital of the province of New Normandy, an autonomous duchy under the French king, Louis Augustus. Great affairs are afoot here, Curlon. Rebels challenge the power of the Emperor, loyalists are charged with treason, and across the Channel, Louis waits, ready to land forces at Harwich and Dover and Newcastle if needed. A touch would send the situation crashing into war. It's that which we must prevent."

"And what's in it for you, General?"

"I'm known here; I enjoy the confidence of both Viceroy Garonne and important members of the rebellious faction.

My hope is to prevent bloodshed, stabilize the situation. A strongly established A-line is necessary to contain the vast energies I've channeled here. You'll recall what I told you of key objects, key lines. New Normandy will become the key line of its probability quantum, with the aid of the artifact we brought here. And with the rise of the new masterline, our stars too will ascend!"

"And where do I come in?"

"Ten days ago, Duke Richard fell dead at a public ceremony in full view of the populace. Murdered, they say. The rebels charge the loyalists with eliminating the natural leader of the Britons; the loyalists in turn charge the rebels with killing a man they regarded as no more than a vassal of the French king. The tension has reached crisis level; it must be relieved."

"I still haven't heard anything illuminating."

"It's really quite obvious," Roosevelt said. "As a Plantagenet born and bred, you'll step forward to take up the role of the Duke of Londres."

"You're out of your mind, General," I told him.

"Nothing could be simpler," he said with a wave of the hand. "No one could deny that you look the part; you're enough like the departed Duke to be his brother. However, we shall present you in the role of a more distant relation, raised secretly north of the Scots border. Your appearance will satisfy the most fanatical rebel, and of course you'll make suitably defiant pronouncements to satisfy that clique. More discreetly, you'll engage in dialogues with Viceroy Garonne aimed at easing the crisis and restoring civil order."

"What's going to make me do all this?"

"This is the drama of life itself—and you were a part of it from the moment you were born—and before. Like me, you're the inheritor of a mighty dynasty. All that you might have been—that your analogs, those close to you might have done—all the vast repercussions across time and history of every act of that great clan, chopped down in the prime of their strength—all those aborted probability energies must find their expression in you—and in the world you help create!"

"What about my own world?"

"The new master-line will dominate the quantum," Roosevelt said flatly. "In the readjustment that accompanies its establishment, lesser lines must of necessity be sacrificed. The Imperium and the Blight Insular lines will go under. But that's a matter of no moment to you, Mr. Curlon—or to me. Our destinies lie elsewhere."

"You have it all figured out," I said. "There's just one weak point."

"Which is?"

"I won't play."

Roosevelt looked grim. "Understand me, Curlon: I want you as my willing ally; but willing or not, you'll help me."

"You're bluffing, Roosevelt. You need a walking, talking puppet, not a man with wires on his wrists."

He made an impatient gesture. "I told you I regretted that, and the need for drugging you to bring you here. But I'd do it again, ten thousand times, if that were the only way! The Old Empire *will* rise again! We're not discussing *if*, Curlon; only *how*. Meet this challenge—lend me your full support—and your future will be of a splendor unimaginable to you now. Defy me, and you'll walk like a corpse through what would have been your triumph. Which do you want, Curlon? Honors, or rotted rags? Majesty, or misery?"

"You've worked your story out pretty carefully, General. But it still doesn't make sense."

"The rebels are strong," Roosevelt said grudgingly. "They have all the strength on their side, if the truth were known. They could seize power any time they chose. They lack only one thing: leadership. They'll rally to you, Curlon—but instead of leading them to victory, you'll cool their revolutionary fervor. Because if they should rise up and cast out the French, a major branching of the line will result! Seven hundred years of stable history would be shattered, creating a whole new probability spectrum. I need not detail the effect this would have on my plans for New Normandy!"

I smiled a smile I didn't feel. "You're in trouble, aren't you, Roosevelt? You need me—and not just to carry a spear in the third act of some farce to fool the locals. What is it? What's the real reason for trying to drag me into this paranoid fantasy-system of yours?"

"I've told you! We're linked, you and I, all down through the corridors of past time, on every world within a thousand years of common history. As your fortunes wax, so do mine. I can force you, Curlon—but to the extent that I must break you to my will our joint stature is diminished. Join with me freely, lend your *mana* to mine—and anything we desire is within our grasp!"

"And if I don't?"

"I want your willing aid," he said in a steely voice. "But your broken mind and body, dangling from the strings, will serve if need be."

"Everything you say confirms the one clear idea I've gotten from all this, Roosevelt. Whatever this fight is, you're on one side, and I'm on the other."

"I can break you, Curlon. The stronger man can always break the weaker. A simple demonstration will suffice to prove my point." He took a stance with his feet apart and raised his arms until they were level with his shoulders, smiling.

"The first to drop his arms acknowledges the other man his superior—at least in one small way."

I put my arms out. The effort made my temples pound, but I didn't burst into tears. If Roosevelt wanted to play little games I was willing to go along. The hamburger machines could wait.

"In every world, in every time, the will of some man has shaped reality," Roosevelt said suddenly. "Here, now, that old rule is still in force—but made more potent by the existence of titanic new forces. Those forces are at the command of whoever can master them. Fate is a fragile thing, Curlon. A mindless thing, controlled by the whim of a strong man. Let an Alexander set out to conquer the world; the world becomes what he makes it. Without Alexander, there would have been no Caesar, no Atilla, no Muhammad, no Hitler in your world, no Guglielmo Maxoni in the Zero-zero line. Men make fate, Curlon, not the other way around. You saw that demonstrated when we fought together, back to back. We two form islands of stability about ourselves, even in a sea of formlessness.

"But only one of us can shape the cosmos to his will. That one will be me. I'll dominate you—not because I hate you—I have no cause for enmity. But because I must—as an Alexander must destroy a Persia."

"Funny," I said, "I never had any interest in shaping the cosmos to my will. But I'm not willing to see it shaped to yours. Home was never much to me, but I'm not ready to see it flushed down the drain to give you a roost to rule."

Roosevelt nodded. "I suppose it's a thing outside both of us, Curlon, written in the stars, as they say. For seven hundred years, your ancestors and mine fought to rule the quantum. Think of it, Plantagenet! In a thousand billion alternate world-lines, each differing from the others in some greater or lesser degree, your clan and mine, striving, down through the centuries, each to dominate his world, none knowing of the others, all driven by the common instinct to fulfill the potentiality inherent in them. And then—the day of cataclysm, when the Blight swept in to wipe them out, root, stem and branch—all but one man of my line, and one of yours."

It had been about ten minutes since the game had begun. Fiery pains were shooting along the backs of my arms and shoulders. Roosevelt was still standing as rigid as a statue. His arms hadn't quivered.

"They tell me the Blight dates back to the nineties," I said. "You're a little young to be remembering it—unless your Imperium has face-lift techniques that beat anything Hollywood's come up with."

"I'm telling you what I've learned—what my researches have revealed, what I was told—" He cut himself off.

"I thought this was all your own idea, Roosevelt."

"Told—by my father," Roosevelt said. "He devoted his life to the conviction that somehow—somewhere—our time would come again. His world was gone—but how could such glory be forever vanished? He worked, studied, and in the end made his discovery. He was old then, but he passed the charge on to me. And I've made it good! I worked first to gain a powerful position within Imperial Intelligence—the one organization that knew the secrets of the Net. This gave me a platform from which to prepare this line—New Normandy—to be the vessel that would contain and shape the forces of the Blight."

I had to concentrate on keeping my arms at shoulder level. Somehow, it seemed important not to lose at Roosevelt's game. If he was suffering, he didn't show it.

"Are you tiring?" he asked in a conversational tone. "Poor Mother Nature, so blind in her efforts to protect the body. She sends pain as a warning, first. Then little by little, she'll numb the nerves. Your arms will begin to sag. You'll try, with all your will, to hold them high—to outdo me, your inevitable master. But you'll fail. Oh, the strength is there—but Nature forces you to husband your strength. So though you might be willing, of yourself, to endure the torture of fatigue until death from exhaustion—she won't let you. You'll suffer—for nothing. A pity, Mr. Curlon."

I was glad he felt like talking. It kept my mind off the hot clamps set in the back of my neck. I tried to fan a little spark of anger alive—another of Mother Nature's tricks, this one on my side. I wanted to keep him chattering, but at the same time coax along the frustration I hoped he was beginning to feel.

"Seeing you drop will be worth waiting for," I said.

"But you won't. I'm stronger than you are, Mr. Curlon.

Since childhood I've trained every day in these exercises—and the mental control that goes with them. At the age of seven I could hold a fencing foil across my palms at arm's length for a quarter of an hour. For me, this is literally child's play. But not for you."

"There's nothing to this," I said breezily. "I can stand here all day."

"So far, you've endured it for less than a quarter of an hour. How will you feel fifteen minutes from now, eh, Mr. Curlon? And half an hour after that?" He smiled—not quite the easy smile he'd have liked. "In spite of yourself, you'll have failed long before then. A simple demonstration, Curlon—but a necessary one. You must be brought to realize that in me you've met your superior."

"There must be a catch to it," I said. "Maybe this is supposed to keep my attention occupied while your pals aim a spy beam at my brains—or whatever it is mad scientists do."

"Don't talk like a fool, Curlon," Roosevelt almost snapped the words. "Or—why, yes, I see." He smiled and the strain went out of his face. "Very good, Mr. Curlon. You were almost beginning to irritate me. A well-designed tactic. Such distractions can appreciably sap endurance. By the way, how are your arms feeling? A trifle heavy?"

"Fine," I said in what I hoped was a light tone. "How about yours?" The lines of fire were lancing out into my trapezius muscles, playing around my elbows, tingling in my fingertips. My head ached. Roosevelt looked as good as new. He stared across at me, silent now. That bothered me. I wanted him to talk.

"Keeping up the patter's hard work, eh? But I'll tip you, Roosevelt. You picked the wrong man. I'm a fisherman. I'm used to fighting the big ones eight hours at a stretch. For me, this is a nice rest."

"A flimsy lie, Curlon. I expect better of you."

"The circulation is the weak point," I said. "Soldiers

who could march all day in the sun under a full pack used to drop out in a dead faint on parade. Standing at attention, not moving, restricted the flow of blood to the brain—and all of a sudden—blackout. Some fellows couldn't take it. Nothing against them, just a peculiarity of the metabolism. It never bothered me. Good circulation, you know. How's yours?"

"Excellent, I assure you."

"But you're not talking." I gave him a grin that cost me a year off the end of my life.

"I've said what I intended."

"I don't believe you. You had canned lecture number three all ready to go. I can see it in your eyes."

Roosevelt laughed—a genuine laugh. "Mr. Curlon, you're a man after my own heart. I wish we could have met in another time at another place. We might have been friends, you and I."

Neither of us said anything after that. I discovered I was counting off the seconds. It had been about twenty minutes now, maybe a little more. I realized one hand was sagging and brought it back up. Roosevelt smiled a faint smile. More time passed. I thought about things, then tried not to think about things. It occurred to me that the ancient Chinese had wasted a lot of time and effort designing iron maidens and chipping bamboo splinters. Torture was a sport you could play without equipment. And Roosevelt's version was a double challenge, because the only one forcing me was me. I could quit now and laugh it off and call for the next round.

That was the catch. There'd be a next round—and one after that. And if I quit on the first, I'd quit sooner on the second, until I refused to meet his challenge—and that was what he wanted.

That was his swindle. To make me think that if I lost—I'd lost. But it wasn't true. Losing was nothing. Only surrender counted.

And once I understood that, I felt better. The pain was like flaying knives, but it was just pain, something to be endured until it ended. I hitched my arms back up into line and stared across at him through the fading light . . .

. . . and came to, lying on the floor. Roosevelt was standing over me. His face looked yellowish and drawn.

"A commendable effort, Curlon," he said. "One hour and twelve minutes. But as you see—you lost. As you must always lose—because it's your destiny to lose to me. Now—will you join with me willingly?"

I climbed back to my feet, feeling dizzy, and with slow fires still burning in my shoulders. I raised my arms to the crucifix position.

"Ready to try it again?" I said. Roosevelt's face twitched before he laughed.

I grinned at him. "You're afraid, aren't you, Roosevelt? You see your grand scheme coming apart at the seams—and you're afraid."

He nodded. "Yes—I'm afraid. Afraid of my own weakness. You see—incredible though it may seem to you—I truly wanted you to be a part of it, Plantagenet. A foolish sentimentality—but you, like me, are a man of the ancient stock. Even a god can be lonely—or a devil. I offered you comradeship. But at the first trial, you turned against me. I should have known then. And now I've learned the lesson. I have no choice left to me. My course is plain now."

"You're a flawed devil, Roosevelt," I said. "A devil with a conscience. I pity you."

He shook his head. "I want none of your pity, Plantagenet. As I can have none of your friendship. What I want from you, I'll take, though the taking will destroy you."

"Or you."

"That's a risk I'll run." He motioned to the waiting guards; they closed in around me. "Spend these next hours in meditation," he said. "Tonight you'll be invested with the honors of a dukedom. And tomorrow you'll be hanged in chains."

2

The dungeons under the viceregal palace were everything that dungeons should be, with damp stone walls and iron doors and unshielded electric lights that were worse than smoky flambeaux. The armed men in Swiss Guard uniforms that had herded me down from the upper levels waited while a burly man with a round, oily, unshaven face opened a barred grill on a six-by-eight stone box with straw. I didn't move fast enough for him; he swung a kick to hurry me along, but it never landed. Roosevelt showed up in time to slam the back of his hand across the fat face.

"You'd treat a royal duke like a common felon?" he barked. "You're not fit to touch the floor he stands on."

Another man grabbed up the fat man's keys, led the way along the narrow passage, opened an oak door on a larger cell with a bed and a loophole window.

"You'll meditate here in peace," Roosevelt told me, "until I have need of you."

I lay on the bed and waited for the pounding in my head to retreat to a bearable level.

... and woke up with a voice that wasn't in my head, whispering, "Plantagenet! Be of good cheer! Wait for the signal!"

3

I lay where I was and waited for more, but there wasn't any more.

"Who's that?" I whispered, but nobody answered. I got up and examined the wall by my head, and the bed itself. It was just a wall, just a bed. I went to the door and listened, pulled myself up and looked out the six-inch slit at a light-well. There were no lines dangling there with files tied to them; no trapdoors opened up in the ceiling. I was locked in a cell, with no way out, and that was that. The voices were probably courtesy of the management, another of Roosevelt's subtle moves to either wear me down or convince me I was crazy. He was doing pretty well on both counts.

4

I was having a fine dream about a place where flowers as big as cabbages grew on trees beside a still lake. Ironel was there, walking toward me across the water, and the water broke into a sea of glass splinters, and when I tried to reach her, the flowers turned to heads that shouted threats and the branches were arms that grabbed at me, and shook me—

Hands shook me awake; lights shone in my face. Men with neat uniforms and unholstered nerve-guns took me along passages and up stairs to a room where Roosevelt waited, rigged out in purple velvet and ermine and loops of gold cord. A jewel-covered sword as big as a cased garrison flag hung at his side as if it belonged there. He didn't talk, and neither did I. Nobody was interested in the condemned man's last words.

Servants clustered around, fitting me with heavy garments of silk and satin and gold thread. A barber trimmed my hair, and poured perfume on me. Someone fitted red leather shoes to my feet. Roosevelt himself strapped a wide, brocaded baldric around my waist, and the tailor's helper attached a jeweled scabbard to it. The hilt that projected from it was unadorned and battered. It was my old knife, looking out of place in all this magnificence. The armorer complained, offered a shiny sword, but Roosevelt waved him away.

"Your sole possession, eh, Curlon?" he said. "It shares

your aura strongly. You'll keep it by you—in your moment of glory."

A procession formed up in the wide corridor outside, with the gun-handlers sticking unobtrusively close to me. Roosevelt was beside me as we walked up a wide staircase into an echoing hall hung with spears and banners and grim-faced paintings. Wigged and spangled and beribboned people filled the room. Beyond an arched opening, I saw a high, stained-glass window above a canopied altar. I knew where I was then.

I was standing in the spot where I had stood with Ironel, with the griffin, Vrodelix, beside us, just before Roosevelt had tried the first time to reach the altar. Now the floor was carpeted in gold rose, and there was an odor of incense in the air, and the woodwork gleamed with the dull shine of wax—but it was the same room—and not the same. Not by a thousand years of history.

We halted, and priests in red robes and dry-faced old men in ribbons and fluffy little wigs went into action, handing ritual objects back and forth, ducking their heads at each other, mumbling incantations. I suppose it was an impressive ceremony, there in the ancient room under the damask-draped, age-blackened beams, but I hardly noticed it. I kept remembering Ironel, leading Roosevelt to her Pretty Place, so that he could destroy it.

The odor of incense was strong; strong enough to burn my eyes. I sniffed harder and realized I was smelling something more than scented smoke; it was the real kind, that comes from burning wood and cloth and paint. There was a faint, brassy haze in the air. Roosevelt was looking back; the head priest interrupted his spiel. The gun-handlers jostled in close to me, looking worried. Roosevelt snapped off some orders, and I heard yells from outside the big room. A wave of heat rolled at us then, and the party broke up. Four guns prodded me toward the archway. If this was a signal, it was a dandy, but there wasn't much I could do about it. The nerve-gun squad cut a path through the notables who were dithering, coughing, half headed one way and half the other. We reached the low steps, and two new guards came in from the flank and there was some fast footwork, and they were close to me, and the crowd was closing around us, fighting for position. An old boy in pink and gold, with his wig askew, thrust his face close to mine.

"Favor the left, y'r Grace," he hissed in my ear. I was still working on that one when I saw the nearest guard put his nerve-gun in his partner's kidney and press the button. Two more men in uniform came from somewhere; I heard a thud behind me, and then we were clear, peeling off from the edge of the main crowd, heading right into the smoke.

"Only a few yards, y'r Grace," the little old man squeaked. A door opened and we were in a cramped stairway, leading down. On the landing, all four guards stripped off their uniform jackets and tossed their caps aside and pulled on workmen's coveralls from a stack behind the door. The old fellow ditched his wig and cape and was in a footman's black livery. They handed me a long gray cloak. The whole operation was like a well-practiced ballet. It didn't take twenty seconds.

On the next floor down, we pushed out into a concourse full of spectators, firemen, a few belted earls and mitred priests, none of them looking at a repair crew in dirty overalls. The old man led the way to a passage where a lone sentry stood, looking anxious. He stepped in front of us, and the old boy raised a finger and drew him around to the right while one of the others expertly sapped him back of the ear. Then we were in the passage and running.

Two startled scrubwomen watched us cross the kitchen and duck out a door between garbage cans into an unlit alley. The truck parked there started up with a lot of valve click and black kerosene exhaust. I went over the tailgate and the old man scrambled up behind me and pulled the canvas flap down as the truck pulled away. Three minutes later, it slowed, stopped. I heard voices up front, the clatter of a gun, leather boots on cobbles. After a minute, gears clashed and we went on. On the bench opposite, my new friend let out a held breath and grinned from ear to ear.

"Worked like a charm," he said. He cackled and rubbed his hands together. "Like a bloody charm, beggin' y'r Grace's pardon."

5

The old man's name was Wilibald. "Our friends are waiting for y'r Grace," he said. "True Britons, they are, every man Jock o' 'em. Simple men, y'r Grace, but honest! Not like those treasonous palace blackguards in their silks and jewels!" He gnashed his gums and wagged his head.

"That was a neat play, Wilibald," I said. "How did you manage it?"

"There's true men among the Bluecoats, y'r Grace. The jailor was one. He tried to lodge y'r Grace in a safe cell—one we'd a tunnel to—but his high and mightiness the Baron would ha' none o't. So it took a little longer. But here y'r Grace be now, all the same!" He cackled and rasped his hands together like a cricket's wings.

"You're with the rebel party?"

"Some call us rebels, y'r Grace—but to honest men, we're patriots, pledged to rid these islands o' the French pox!"

"Why did you spring me?"

"Why? Why?" the old man looked astonished. "When word went abroad the Plantagenet was housed in the viceregal tombs, what other course could a loyal Briton follow, y'r Grace? Did y'r Grace deem we'd leave ye there to rot?"

"But I'm not—" I started and left it hanging.

"Not what, y'r Grace?" Wilibald asked. "Not surprised? Of course not. There's ten million Britons in this island, sworn to free the land o' tyranny!"

"Not going to waste any time," I finished. "We'll strike immediately."

6

The traffic on the road was a mixed bag of horse carts, big solid-tired trucks with open cabs, little droop-snoot cars that looked as if they came in cereal boxes and more than a sprinkling of blue-painted military vehicles. According to Wili, the viceroy was concentrating his forces around the fortified ports, ready to cover the landing of reinforcements if the talk of rebellion crystalized into action. The place we were headed for was the country seat of Sir John Lackland.

"A dark-avised gentleman," Wili said. "But moneyed, and of the ancient stock." He rambled on for the next hour, filling me in on the local situation. The rebels, he swore, were ready to move. And according to Roosevelt, if they moved, they'd win.

"You'll see," Wili told me. "Loyal Britons will rise to a man and flock to y'r Grace's standard!"

After an hour's run, we turned down a side road and swung in between brick pillars, went along a drive that led through tended woods into a cobbled yard fronting a three-story house with flower boxes and leaded windows and half-timbered gables that looked like the real thing. Steps went up to a broad veranda. An old man in a fancy vest and black pants and house slippers let us in. His eyes bugged when he saw me.

" 'Is Grace must see Sir John at once," Wili said.

"Sir John's been abed this twoday wi' a touch o' the ague. He's had no callers—"

"He has now," Wili cut him off.

The old fellow dithered, then led the way into a dark room full of books, and shuffled away.

I looked at the books on the shelves, mostly leather-bound volumes with titles like *Historic Courts* and *Campaigns Among the Quanecticott*. After five minutes or so the door opened and the old fellow was back, piping that Sir John would see us now.

The master of the house was in a bedroom on the top floor, a lean-faced sharp-nosed old aristocrat with a silky black eyebrow-moustache and a matching fringe of hair around a high bald dome. He was propped up in a bed no larger than a skating rink, half buried in a violet satin pillow with an embroidered monogram and more lace than a Hollywood bishop. He had a tan woolen bathrobe with satin lapels wrapped around him, and a knitted shawl over that, and even so, the end of his nose looked cold. When he saw me, he nearly jumped out of bed.

"What—how . . . ?" he stared from me to Wili and back. "Why did you come here—of all places?"

"Where else would I be more likely to find friends?" I came back.

"Friends? I'd heard that the viceregent had declared a pretender heir to the dukedom, but I scarce expected to see him present himself *here* in that guise."

"How do you know I'm the man—or that I'm an imposter?"

"Why—why—who else would you be?"

"You mean you're accepting me as genuine? I'm glad, Sir John. Because the time has come for action."

"Action? What action?"

"The liberation of Briton."

"Are you mad? You'd bring destruction down on my house—on all of us! We Plantagenets have always lived on sufferance! The murder of Duke Richard shows us all how precarious our position is—"

"Who killed him?"

"Why—Garrone's men, of course."

"I wonder about that. From the viceroy's point of view,

it was a foolish move. It aligned the Britons against him more solidly than Richard ever did alive."

"Conjecture. Idle conjecture," Sir John barked. "You come here, unbidden, preaching treason! What do I know about you? You imagine I'll place our trust in an upstart, a stranger?"

"Hardly that, Sir John," Wili said indignantly. "One glance at him—"

"What do you know of him, fellow? Is any oversized carrot-locked bumpkin who cares to lay claim to the dukedom to be accepted without question?"

"That's hardly fair, Sir John—"

"Enough! The matter will have to wait for resolution until I can summon certain influential men! In the meantime, I'll give you sanctuary. I can do no more." Lackland gave me a look like a dagger in the ribs and yanked at his bellcord. The old footman popped in with a speed that suggested he'd been standing by not far away.

"Show milord to his suite," Lackland got out between lips as stiff as a Hoover collar. "And quarter Master Wilibald below stairs."

I followed my guide along the corridor to a high-ceilinged, airy room with big windows and a sitting room and bath opening from it. The old fellow showed me the soap and towel and then paused at the door and gave me a sly look.

"It did me heart proud to hear y'r honor gi' a bit o' the rough to his Lordship," he cackled. "It's been a weary time since a real fighting duke put foot o' these old boards, beggin' y'r Honor's pardon."

"You listen at keyholes, eh?" But I grinned at him. "Wake me as soon as the clan's gathered. I wouldn't want to miss anything."

"Rely on me, y'r Grace," he said and went out and I pulled off my boots and lay in the dark and slid off into a dream about knights on horseback riding with leveled lances into the fire of massed machine guns.

7

I came back from somewhere a long way off with a hand shaking my shoulder and a thin old voice saying, "They're here, y'r Grace! Milord Lackland's wi' 'em i' the study this minute—and unless I mistake me, there's mischief afoot!"

"Does Lackland know you're here?"

"Not 'im, y'r Grace."

We went down the stairs and across the hall to a door that was standing ajar. When Wili got close he turned and gave me a quick jerk of the head, cupping his ear.

". . . imposter, gentlemen," Lackland was saying. "No true Briton, but a hireling of Garrone, bought with French gold and sent here to betray us all—"

I pushed the door open and walked in. The talk cut off as if a switch had been thrown. There were about a dozen men grouped around a long table with Lackland seated at the head. They were dressed in a variety of costumes, but all of them featured fur and brocades and a sword slung at the hip. The nearest was a big, wide-shouldered, neckless man with a curly black beard and ferocious eyes. He took a step back when he saw me, looked me up and down, surprised.

"Don't be beguiled by his face and stature!" Lackland spat the words. "He'd seize control of the rebellion, and turn coat, come to terms with Garrone! Can he deny it?" He was pointing at me with a finger that quivered with rage.

I didn't answer immediately. What he was saying was precisely what Roosevelt had proposed. There seemed to be a message for me in that somewhere, but it wouldn't come clear.

"You see?" Lackland crowed. "The treacher dares not deny it!"

The black-bearded man drew his sword with a skin-crawling rasp.

105

"A shrewd stroke!" he said in a high, rasping voice. "With a Plantagenet puppet to dance on his strings, he'd accomplish what the Louis have dreamed of for seven centuries! The total subjugation of Briton!" More swords were out now, ringing me in.

"Spit him, Tudor!" Lackland screeched.

"Stop!" Wilibald stood in the doorway with fire in his old eye. "Would you murder our Duke in cold blood? In the name of Free Briton, I say he deserves a better hearing at your Lordships' hands than this!"

For an instant, nobody moved—and in the silence I heard a droning sound, far away but coming closer. The others heard it, too. Eyes swiveled to stare at the ceiling as if they could see through it. A man rushed to the window, threw back the long drapes to stare out. Another jumped for a wall switch. Tudor didn't move as the chandelier went dark, leaving just what light filtered in from the hall.

"An aircraft!" a man at the window called. "Coming straight in over us!"

"It was a trick to get us here together!" a lean man in yellow snarled, and drew back his sword for a cut. I saw this from the corner of my eye; it was Tudor I was watching. His jaw had set harder, and the tendons beside his neck tensed and I knew the thrust was coming.

I twisted sideways and leaned back and the point ripped through the ruffles on the front of my shirt; my backhanded swing caught him across the cheekbone, knocked him backward into the table as the room went pitch dark. The engines sounded as if they were right down the chimney. A piece of bric-a-brac fell from the mantle.

The *to-to! to-to!* marched across off to the right and the engine sound was deafening, and then receding. I heard glass tinkling, but the ceiling didn't fall in. I slid along the wall toward the door and heard feet break for it and a chair went over. Somebody slammed into me and I grabbed him and threw him ahead of me. I found the door and got through it, and could see the big hall faintly by the moonlight coming through the stained glass along the gallery. There was a lot of yelling that was drowned by the bomber's engines. Then a flash lit the room and the wall seemed to jump outward about a foot. When things stopped falling, I was bruised, but still alive. Wilibald was lying a few feet away, covered with dust and brick chips. There was a timber across his legs above the ankle; by the time I got it clear the plane was making its third run. With the old man over my shoulder, I reached the rear hall just as the front of the house blew in. I made it out through the kitchen door, went across grass that was littered with bricks. Blood from a cut on my scalp was running into my eyes. I made it to a line of trees before my legs folded.

The roof was gone from the house and flames were leaping up a hundred feet high and boiling into smoke clouds that glowed orange on their undersides. The shells of the walls that were still standing stood up in black silhouetted against the fire, and the windows were bright orange rectangles cut in the black.

Then there was a sound and I tried to get up and made it as far as my hands and knees, and three men with singed beards and torn finery and bare swords in their hands came out of the darkness to surround me.

One of the men was Tudor; he stepped in close and drew his arm back, and I was bracing myself for the thrust when all three of them turned and looked toward the house. Light flickered from among the trees lining the drive; pieces of bark jumped from the bole of the tree beside me and the man nearest it went over backward and the man beside him spun and fell, and Tudor turned to run, but it was the wrong reflex. I saw the bullets smack into him, throw him six feet onto his face.

There were men on the drive, coming up at a run—men in blue uniforms. I started to crawl and suddenly old Wilibald was there, his thin hair wild, soot on his face. He had been below the line of fire, like me; he was all right.

"Run, Wili!" I yelled. He hesitated for a moment, then turned and disappeared into the woods. Then the soldiers were all around me, grim and helmeted, smoking guns ready. And I waited for what came next.

Chapter Ten

This time, I got to ride up front. The countryside was pretty, but the towns were as deserted as Mexican villages at siesta time. You could feel in the air that a storm was about to break, and the populace had taken cover. If the rebels were as strong as Roosevelt said, it didn't show. The roads were full of military traffic in the blue paint of the French king. I wondered how much my short-lived escape had to do with that. I tried to pump the man beside me, but he didn't answer.

When we rolled into the outskirts of Londres, the town was carrying on some semblance of business as usual. The shops were open, and big canvas-topped buses rumbled along the streets, half full. We passed a big market square, lined with stalls with bright-colored awnings and displays of flowers and vegetables. At one side a raised platform was roped off. Half a dozen downcast-looking men and women in drab gray stood there, under a sign above the platform that said BULLMAN & WINDROW—CHATTELS. It was a slave market.

We swung into a cobbled courtyard ringed in by high walls. I was hustled inside, along a corridor full of the smell of government offices.

An officer in shirt-sleeves stepped out of a door ahead, swiveled hard when he saw me. He rattled off a question in strange-sounding French that sounded like "Where are you taking him?"

"*A la général, mon major.*"

"*No, c'est la province du demiregent. Laissez les cordes!*"

"*J'ai les ordeurs direct—*"

"A diable avec vos ordeurs! Fait que je dit, vite!"

The sergeant in charge of my detail put a hand on his holstered pistol. The major shouted to someone inside the room. Two sharp-looking lads in khaki with holstered side arms appeared behind him. That ended the argument. One of the new men cut the ropes off. Then they formed up a new procession and marched me off in a new direction.

We rode up in an elevator, went along a lushly carpeted hall, into a fancy outer office. A young fellow in a shiny blue uniform with aide's aglets ducked in through the inner door, came back and made an ushering motion to me. I walked through and was looking at Garonne, the French viceroy.

2

He was a pouch-eyed fellow in his late forties or early fifties, with thick gray hair, a large, rather soft-looking mouth with a quirk at one end registering benign intentions grown weary. He wore Ben Franklin glasses over a pair of sharp black eyes. His clothes were plain, his fingers lean and competent and without rings.

"I regret the discomfort you were forced to undergo, milord," he said, in straight New Norman without a trace of French accent. His voice was deep as a bullfrog's. "In view of the great importance of time just now, I asked that you be brought directly to me. A discussion between us might yet retrieve the unfortunate situation that now obtains."

"How does Baron General van Roosevelt feel about that?" I asked. It didn't mean anything. I was just probing.

"Some of my lieutenants are overzealous," he said cryptically. "It is a matter I must deal with. However, the business of the moment takes precedence. I am empowered, your Grace, by His Most Christian Majesty, to offer certain emoluments to loyal liegemen who support his efforts to calm the present unrest. Among them, greater internal autonomy for the island, with offices to deserving servants; various tax and import benefits, revised trade regulations, including issuance of import licenses to men of proven character. For yourself, a royal patent as Prince Imperial of the New Normandy provinces, together with the grant of estates and pensions appropriate to your station. And of course, full recognition of your status as inheritor of the ancient honors of your House."

"What do I do to earn all this?" I stalled.

"You will accept appointment, under his Majesty, as emergency peace marshal of New Normandy. You will appear on telescreen and wireless and instruct all loyal New Normans to return to their homes, and exhort all subjects of his Majesty to observe his laws regarding assembly and bearing of arms. In short, only those acts which I feel certain your own good judgment would dictate, once freed from the pressures placed on you by incendiary elements: the exercise of your influence toward the achievement of civil stability and order."

"In other words, just sell out the Britons."

Garonne narrowed his eyes at me. He leaned across the desk. "Don't waste my time. I'm sure you'll find my offer preferable to a miserable death in the interrogation section."

"You wouldn't murder me, Monsieur Garonne," I said, trying to sound as if I believed it. "I'm the people's hero, remember?"

"We can drop all that nonsense between us," Garonne said in a flat tone. "I'm aware of your masquerade. There was no Lady Edwinna, no secret hideaway in Scotland, no long-lost heir of the bastard honors of Plantagenet! Who are you? Where do you come from? Who sent you here?"

3

"Whoever I am," I said, "you need me all in one piece."
"Nonsense. Modern methods of persuasion don't rely on

thumbscrews. In the end you'll babble whatever I choose for you to babble. But if you'll act as I command—now—lives will be saved. His Majesty's offer still stands. Now, again: Who are you? Who sent you?"

"If I'm a fake, what makes you think what I say will help you?"

"Rumors of your presence are abroad here—a Plantagenet of the Old Mark, as Duke Richard was, but without his shabby record of failure and compromise. If word spreads that you've been killed, the countryside will rise—and I'll have no choice but to crush the revolt."

"That might not be easy. The guerrillas—"

"There are no guerrillas, no irregulars, no rebel organization. These are fictions, fabricated by myself." He nodded. "Yes, myself. Consider the facts: New Normandy has been the scene of increasing unrest for decades now, most particularly since the Continental War of 1917-1919, with its Prussian dirigible raids, and the less than glorious peace that ended it. The old cries of Saxon unity were revived—idiotic nonsense, of course, based on imaginary blood-ties. I needed a force which would bring the provinces back under tight control. Duke Richard was the perfect foil. By his loose living, he had discredited himself with the islanders, of course—but a rousing call to ancient loyalties served to unite popular sentiment behind him. Then—with all New Normandy pledged to follow him—the final stroke would have been the 'compromise,' granting the hollow honors he craved—and placating the revolutionary spirit with fancied autonomy. His murder destroyed a scheme ten years in the building."

"You murdered him yourself."

"No. It was not I who killed him! He was a valuable tool—and unless you—whoever you are, whatever your original intentions—can be brought to see the wisdom of cooperation—I foresee tragedy!"

"You have proof of this?"

"I have Duke Richard's seal on the secret agreement between us. I have the records of payments to him, of subsidies to him and to various *agents provocateurs* working ostensibly for his underground organization. Of course, they might be counterfeit—how can I demonstrate otherwise? My best evidence is the inherent logic of my version of affairs, as opposed to the romantic nonsense you've been deluded into accepting! Face facts, man! You have the opportunity laid at your feet to spring from obscurity to princely rank overnight. Your best—your *only* interest lies in cooperation!"

"I don't believe you. The rebels can win."

"Nonsense!" He pointed to a wall map, showing blue arrows aimed across the channel from Dunkirk to Brest.

"His Majesty's forces are overwhelmingly powerful. The only result of war would be a murderous guerrilla delaying action, profitable to no one."

"Why not give the Britons their independence and save all that?"

Garonne was wagging his head in a weary negative. "Milord, what you propose is, has always been, an economic and political fantasy. These islands, by their very nature, are incapable of pursuing an independent existence. Their size alone would preclude any role other than that of starveling dependent, incapable of self-support, at the mercy of any power which might choose to attempt annexation. A Free Briton, as the fanatics call it, is a pipe dream. No, milord: France will never give up her legitimate interests here. In conscience, she cannot. To discuss such fantasies is a waste of valuable time. You've heard His Majesty's most gracious offer. As we sit here, time is passing—time that takes us closer to the brink of tragedy with each instant. Accept His Majesty's generosity, and in an hour you'll be installed in your own apartments in the town, secure in your position as chief local magistrate of New Normandy, with all the honors and privileges appertaining thereunto; refuse your duty to your soverign, and your end will be a miserable one! The choice is yours, milord!"

He was staring across the desk at me, waiting. The ormolu clock on the marble mantel behind him ticked loudly in the silence. Things were coming at me too fast; there was something I was missing, or forgetting. I needed time to think.

The door opened; a small, dried-up footman with a little white peruke and ribbons on his knees came into the room. He doddered across to the table beside the big desk, put a tray down on it. There was a squat brown bottle, a pair of long-stemmed glasses, a big white napkin folded into a peak. The old fellow lifted the napkin, and scooped a small, flat automatic pistol from under it. He turned and fired three shots into Garonne's chest from a distance of six feet.

4

I saw the stiff black brocade of the viceroy's coat jump as the bullets hit, saw splinters of pinkish mahogany fly from the chair back, heard the dull smack of the slugs as they lodged in the plaster. The pistol had made a soft unimportant sound as it fired: a silencer, or maybe compressed gas. Garonne jerked and threw his arms up and flopped forward with his face on the fancy leather-bound blotter. The old man pulled off the peruke and I saw it was Wilibald. He shrugged out of the long-skirted coat, all gold and blue with little pink flowers. He was wearing plain gray under it, not too clean. He grinned a toothless grin and said, "We'd best be off direct, m'lord." He tucked the gun away and went past me, around the end of the desk where a brilliant scarlet stain was growing, and pulled back the drapes gathered at the end of the big window. There was a dark opening in the paneled wall behind them. His flashlight beam showed me rough brickwork and time-blackened timber, a narrow pasasge leading off into darkness.

"This way, y'r Grace. No time to waste!" There was a sharp note in his voice; an impatient note. I hadn't moved since the shots were fired.

"What's your hurry, Wili?" I said. "No one's going to burst in on the viceroy, in conference—except maybe a trusted servant with his ten o'clock tea."

"How's that? Beggin' y'r Grace' pardon—but that's a dead man lying there! The penalty for murder is hanging! If y'r caught here—"

I went to him and instead of going past him into the passage I caught his wrist.

"What if we're both caught here, Wili? Would that spoil the scheme?"

"We'd hang!" He tried to jerk free, but I held him.

"They all know I was with him. When he's found dead, it will be an open-and-shut case, eh, Wili?"

"What matter if it is? Ye'll be far away by then—"

"Who are you working for, Wili? Roosevelt? He *let* me escape last time, didn't he? Why? So I could stir up the populace? Why did he bomb Lackland's house? But it was a fake raid, wasn't it? Just a flock of near misses—with the machine guns to clean up the witnesses, including Lackland."

"It was Lackland called the attack down on the house!" Wili croaked. "He was a creeping spy and telltale for the Louis, hoping to see y'r Grace killed—but he paid for his crimes! Aye, he paid—"

"Don't kid me—he was working for Roosevelt. I guess he'd outlived his usefulness."

"Shameful times we've fell on," Wili babbled on. "But what was he but a Black Plantagenet, eh? But now it's needful we make our escape. I've a car waiting—"

"Very convenient, you and your cars. It hardly fits in what I've seen of the Organization here. I suppose we'll breeze right through the police lines, just like we did last time, thanks to Roosevelt."

"The Organization—"

"Is a lot of hot air, Wili. Roosevelt sent you here to kill Garonne, and arranged for it to look as though I'd done the job—just as he killed Duke Richard and spread the word Garonne was guilty. Why? The situation was already balanced on a knife-edge. Why did he tell me the rebels had the winning hand? That was another lie. They're evenly matched at best. But he wants them to make their try, wants to see the country cut to pieces in a civil war that won't end until both factions are ruined. Why, again?"

"Y'r daft!" Wili yelped. "Let go, you fool! They'll be here at any instant—"

"Who tipped them this time, you? Better start talking, Wili—and it had better be good—"

I was watching his free hand; it dipped to his pocket and I grabbed it as it came out with the automatic. He was strong, but I was lots stronger.

"I'm going to spoil the play, Wili," I told him. "I'm a little slow, but after awhile even I catch on. Your boss has been dancing me on the strings from the beginning, hasn't he? Every move has been planned: getting me here on my own initiative, the dramatic escape complete with voices coming out of the walls, then letting Garonne's men have me. What's planned for me next? Maybe I'm supposed to get on a horse and lead the peasants into battle, is that it? But I'm breaking the chain, Wili. The moves are too subtle for me, but that doesn't matter. A fancy knot cuts as easy as a simple one—"

His knee came up, almost fast enough. As I took it on the thigh, he put everything he had into twisting the gun around. It wasn't enough. The muzzle was pointing to his own chest when it coughed. He went slack, fell backward into the room. He tried, tried hard to speak, but I couldn't make out the words. Then his eyes went dull and blank. I dragged the body into the passage, felt over the wall until I found the lever that closed the panel behind me.

"Good-bye, Wili," I said. "You were loyal to something,

even if it was the wrong thing." I left him there and started off in what I hoped was the right direction.

5

It was different, picking my way in the dark through the network of hidden passages that I had traced out once before in the shuttle, on half-phase. I made a wrong turning, bumped my head and barked my shins, retraced my steps and tried again. It took me hours—I don't know how many—to find the passage I was looking for: the one that led to Roosevelt's quarters.

I found the lever and eased the panel back and was looking down from over the fireplace into the quiet luxury of the spacious study. It was empty. Roosevelt would be fully occupied elsewhere for a while, working out an explanation of the locked-door murder of the viceroy.

It was a difficult room to search. Every door and drawer was locked, and there were a lot of them. I levered them open one by one, looked at books and papers and boxed records, and drew a blank.

The next rroom was the Baron's sleeping chamber. I started in the closet, worked my way through two large bureaus and a wardrobe, and in the last drawer, found a flat, paper-wrapped bundle. It was my broken sword. I wondered what it meant to Roosevelt that had made him squirrel it away here, but that was a problem I could solve later—maybe. I buckled it on, and the weight of it felt good at my hip. It wasn't much of a weapon, but it was better than nothing, if they walked in and found me here.

Ten minutes later, in a cubicle almost hidden in a shadowy corner, I found what I was looking for: the silver-mounted reliquary box that Roosevelt had destroyed a world to get.

There was a silver lock on the silver hasp that closed the lid. I hated to destroy such a handsome piece of workmanship, but I put the edge of the sword under it and levered and it shattered. The lid came up; inside, in a bed of yellowed satin, lay a rusted slab of steel, a foot long, three inches wide, beveled on both edges. It was another piece of the broken sword.

I picked it up, felt the same premonitory tingle in my hand that I'd felt that other time, in the underground room beneath the old chateau. Like that time, I brought the scrap of metal to the broken blade, saw the long, blue spark jump between them as they came together—

The world exploded in my face.

6

I sat astride a great war-horse, in the early morning. I felt the weight of the chain armor on my back, the drag of the new-forged sword at my side. Beside me, Trumpington turned in his saddle to look across at me. He spoke, but I gave him no answer. A strange vision was on me. Though I was here, a part of me was elsewhere, observing. . . .

My vision widened, and I seemed to see myself riding away from the field of Chaluz, my mind unbloodied. More ghostly images flocked in my mind. I saw the lean face of John my brother, hungry-eyed, silky-bearded, as he knelt before me, pleading for his life. And the sudden look of fear, as I, who had always before been merciful of his treacheries, hardened my heart.

I heard the thunk of the headsman's ax . . .

Then it seemed I sat in my pavilion on the island of Runnymede, summoned there by my rebellious barons. They stood before me in their arrogance, and presented to me, their sovereign lord, the perfidious writing of their demands. And again, I saw their looks of triumph change to the knowledge of death as my hidden bowmen stepped forth and loosed their clothyard shafts into the false hearts of my forsworn vassals . . .

Scenes of warfare passed before my eyes. I saw the walls

of Paris go down before me, saw the fires that blazed up from the cathedrals of Madrid, saw the head of him who once had been a king, impaled on a pike and borne before me. Faces crowded around me, fair women and ambitious men, praising me. There was revelry, and riding behind the baying hounds, and roasted venison before the roaring blaze; and tuns of wine broached, and the passing of days, years of gluttony and lechery and sloth, until the time when my hand no longer sought the sword. Swollen with excess, rotten with disease, I cowered in my palace while my picked retainers parleyed with the invaders at my gates. Parleyed with the invaders at my gates. Parleyed, and sold their kingdom and its king for their own vile lives. But no viler than mine, when I knelt, weeping, at the feet of the stripling whose father I had hanged to his own gates, and swore to him on my sword the eternal servility of all my house . . .

7

I swam back from across a gulf wider than the Universe and was standing in the room I remembered from an eon—or a second—before. The sword burned hot in my hand—no longer an awkward stub, but a blade four feet long, ending in a blunt, broken tip. The cross-guard was different: longer, the quillons curving out above carved knuckle-bows. There were traces of gold on the grip, and a single jewel glinted in the pommel. It was the same magic I'd seen before, all the talk in the world about probability stresses and the reshaping of reality couldn't make it anything else for me. I groped after the dream that had filled my head a moment before: a panorama of faces and sounds and vain regrets; but it faded, as dreams do, and was gone. Then my reverie was shattered into small pieces as the door to the next room slammed open and feet came across the rug toward the bedroom.

"Milord Baron," a familiar voice called. "An emergency in the Net! The stasis has been broken! The probability storm will strike within hours!"

His rush had carried him past me where I had flattened myself to the wall beside the door. He halted when he saw the room was empty, spun, saw me, yelled.

"Thanks for the information, Renata," I said, and laid the flat of the sword against the side of his head with all the power in my arm. I didn't wait to see if I had broken his skull. I went across the study and was back inside my private tunnel before the first of his men had gotten up his nerve to enter without knocking.

8

An hour or two of exploring the tunnel system turned up plenty of side-branches, some secret rooms with tables and rotted bedding, a cramped stairway leading down to ground level; but there seemed to be no direct way into the other wing of the palace and the exit behind the rhododendrons. I thought about coming out and trying it in the open, but there were too many sounds of activity beyond the walls to make that seem really attractive. The whole building seemed to be in a state of uproar. That wasn't too hard to understand. With a dead viceroy to handle, and a probable storm coming on, it looked like a busy day.

My break came when I found a shaft with a rusty ladder bolted inside it.

The rungs were too close together, and scaled with rust, and the bore was barely big enough to give me operating space. It seemed to get smaller as I went down. It ended on a damp floor that I recognized as running behind the rank of cells where I'd once been a guest. I started along the two-foot-wide passage, in near pitch-dark. What light there was came from chinks in the mortar between the stones. If night fell while I was still here, the going would be rough.

I followed the passage fifty feet to a dead end. I turned back, and after thirty feet, encountered an intersection that I would have sworn hadn't been there two minutes before. The right-hand branch led to an uncovered pit that I discovered by almost falling in it. The other spiraled down, debouched into a circular room lined with dark openings. I turned my back, and when I looked again, everything had changed. This time I was sure; where the passage I had entered by had been there was a solid wall of stone. I knew now what Roosevelt meant by a probability storm. Subjective reality had turned as insubstantial as a dream.

The next passage I tried ended in a blank wall of wet clay. When I came back into the circular room it was square, and there were only two exits now. One led to a massive iron-bound door, locked and barred. I retraced my steps, but instead of a room I came into a cave with water trickling across its floor and a single dark opening on the far side. I went into it, and it widened and was a carpeted hall, faced with white doors, all locked. When I looked back, there was only a gray tunnel, cut through solid rock.

For a long time, I wandered through dark passages that closed behind me, looking for a way up. And then, in a tunnel so low that I had to duck my head, I heard the clank of chains, not far away.

I listened hard, heard heavy breathing, the rasp of feet on stone, another clank. It wasn't what would ordinarily be considered an inviting sound, but under the circumstances I was willing to take the risk. I pushed ahead ten feet and saw dim light coming through a crack in the wall. It was a loose stone slab, three feet on a side. I put my eye to the crack and looked into a cell with windowless walls, a candle on a table, a straw pallet. An old man stood in the center of the room. He was as tall as I was, wide through the shoulders, with big, gnarled hands, a weather-beaten complexion, pale blue eyes with a hunted look. He was dressed in tattered blue satin knee-pants, a wine and rose brocaded coat with wide fur lapels, a flowered vest, scuffed and worn shoes that had once been red. The chains were on his ankles. He looked around, scanning the walls as if he knew I was there.

"Geoffrey," he said, in a hoarse, old voice that I'd heard before, in a dream, "I feel you near me."

I got a grip on the stone and slid it aside and was looking through a barred opening. The old man turned slowly. His mouth opened and closed.

"Geoffrey," he said. "My boy . . ." He put out a hand, then drew it back. "But my boy is dead," he told himself. "Forever dead." A tear ran down the leathery cheek. "Who are you, then? His cousin, Henry? Or Edward? Name yourself, then!"

"Curlon is my name. I'm lost. Is there a way out of here?"

He ignored the question. "Who sent you here? The black-hearted rogues who slew Geoffrey?" He caught at the bars, and the sleeve of his coat fell back. There was a welted, two-inch-wide scar all the way around his wrist.

"No one sent me," I said. "I managed it on my own."

He stared at me and nodded. "Aye—you're of the blood—I see it in your face. Are you, too, caught in his traps?"

"It looks that way," I said. "Who are you? Why are you here?"

"Henry Planget is my name. I claim no other honor. But I'll not fall in with his schemes, though all the devils in hell come to haunt me!" He shook his fist at the wall. "Do your damnedest, rascals! But spare the boy!"

"Snap out of it, old man!" I said roughly. "I need your help! Is there a way out of here?"

He didn't answer. I drew the broken sword and levered at the bars. They were solid, an inch thick, set in barred sockets.

"My help?" His rheumy eyes held on mine. "A Planget never calls for help—and yet . . . and yet, perhaps it would have been better if we had, so long ago . . ."

"Listen, to me, Henry. There's a man called Roosevelt—Baron General Pieter van Roosevelt. He's crazy enough to think he can remake the Universe according to a private set of specifications and I'm crazy enough to believe him. I'd like to stop him, if I can. But first, I have to break out of this maze. If you know the way—tell me!"

"The maze?" The old man looked at me vaguely; then as if he were shaking off a weight, he straightened his back; his eyes cleared and vitality came into them.

"The maze of life," he said. "The maze of fate. Yes, we must break out!" He stopped, staring at the broken sword. His hand went out to it, but stopped, not touching it.

"You bear Balingore?" his voice quavered. His eyes met mine, and now fire flashed in them. "A miracle passes before my eyes! For these same eyes saw Balingore broken and cast into the sea! And now . . . he lives again!"

"I'm afraid it's just a broken sword," I said, but he wasn't listening.

"Balingore lives again!" he quavered. "His strength runs in you, lad! I sense it! And still the powers draw at you across the veils of the worlds! I've seen them—yes, he showed me, long ago, when he plied me with fine words and talk of glories vanished. There are more worlds than one, and they call to me—and to you, too! Can you feel them, the voices that cry out of darkness, summoning you? Go! Go to them! Break the ring of fate that forever doomed our house!"

"How do I do that, Henry?"

He clung to the bars and I could see the fight he was having to hold to the glimmer of sanity that had come to him—if that was what it was.

"I must speak quickly, before the veils descend again," he said. His voice was steadier now. "This is the tale that he told me:

"Long ago, a king of our line bore Balingore into battle,

and with him built a mighty empire across the world. But in the end, he turned aside from honor. Balingore passed to the hands of another, and for seven centuries, served the cause of evil. But at last the usurper's greed undid him. His wise men built a strange machine in which a man might leave his proper frame of fate and walk in worlds of might-have-been. He sought to use this wonder as a weapon, to spread his black dream of empire—but he failed. And in his failure, he brought down the very skies about him!"

"The machine was called a shuttle," I said. "It used the MC-drive to move across the alternate world-lines. I've heard that the Blight was caused by the drive running out of control."

"Nay—it was no accidental havoc! Van Roosevelt knew what he did when he unleashed its power on the world! And now his spawn seeks again to mold the cosmos to his liking! But this is a task too great for him alone! He needs the might of Angevin beside him. This much he told me when he snatched me from my manor house in the far world of my birth. But I defied him! As you must!"

"Who is he, Henry? What is he?"

"A fallen angel; a man so evil that the world cannot contain his malice! Even now it melts and flows—as I have seen it melt and flow before! Run, lad! Flee this pit of horrors before you find yourself forever lost . . . as I was lost, so long ago . . ."

"You were telling me about the sword," I reminded him.

"Many things have I learned, strange beyond belief," Henry mumbled. "And yet you must believe them!" The fire came back into his tone. "There are many worlds, many lines of fate that grow across the walls of time like so many vines of ivy! Once there were many Balingores, each holding some fraction of the power that was once welded into one. But in the disaster that overtook the world, all were lost, save two: One, in the hands of the devil, Roosevelt. And another, which hung on the high wall of my house, in a far land I shall never see again!" Knuckles whitened as he gripped the bars. "Once, this was my house, these chambers my cellars. Then *he* came. His talk beguiled me, in my ignorance. At his behest, I took down the ancient blade of my ancestors, and would have put it in his hand. But at his touch, it shattered.

"He raged, blamed me for the miracle. But I took new pride from the sign given me. I defied him, then! Too late, I defied him! He brought me here, told me his tale—and his lies. He swore I was the key to his greatness, that together we would rebuild his world—that other world, so like mine, and yet so different. I would not listen. I saw the sword he bore—the other Balingore, so long ago dishonored—but I sensed that the true power flowed not in it. He needed me, in truth—but what he did not know was that I had saved one fragment of the true sword. I hid it away from him, and when he scattered the shards in the salt sea, there to corrode to nothing, one piece was left behind . . ."

"There were more than two Balingores," I said. "I have part of one. And I found another part, in a ruined city in the Blight—"

"Listen to me!" Henry's voice shook. "I feel the red darkness returning! Time is short! Go to my world, Curlon! Find my house of the high stone walls and the red towers; and there, in the chapel dedicated to St. Richard, search beneath the altar-stone. But beware the False Balingore! Now go—before the world melts away into a tortured dream!"

"I'll try, Henry," I said. "But I can't leave you here. I'll try to find something—some way to release you." I went back along the passage, feeling of the walls, with the vague idea I might find a ring of keys hanging there; but there was nothing.

When I came back to the barred window, the candle still burned on the table; but the room was empty. Only the rusted shackles lay on the floor among scattered bones.

9

For a long time, I stood in the dark, watching the candle burn down and gutter out. Then I went on. I don't know how many hours later it was that I came into a room where light filtered down from a heavy oak door, half-smashed from its hinges. I went up stone steps into late afternoon light in a kitchen that looked as though it had been fought through. There was shooting going on outside, not far away.

The door opened into a bricked alley under high walls. A dead man in a blue uniform lay on his back a few feet from it. I picked up his gun and moved up to cross the street without any unnecessary noise. In the distance, big guns rumbled and boomed, and flashes showed against the colors of early dusk. I knew where I was now. I had covered several city blocks, underground. The viceregal palace was in the next square, a hundred yards away.

A sudden burst of gunfire nearby made me flatten myself against the wall. I heard running feet, and three blue-uniformed Imperial guards dashed out of a doorway, heading across the street. There was more gunfire, from up high, and one of them fell. A shell shrieked, and a section of street blew up and blanketed the scene with dust. When it cleared, a dead civilian with a bandolier across his shoulders lay near the dead soldier. The revolution was in full swing, but somehow I had a feeling that in spite of that, things hadn't turned out the way Roosevelt had wanted them. The thought warmed me, and turned my mind to what I had to do next.

I left my cubbyhole, made it across the street, and into a narrow street that led to the delivery yard at the back of the palace. I went along it with the machine pistol ready; I didn't want to be gunned down, by either side. Near the gate, I heard feet coming up behind me. I threw the gun away and went over the wall and was in the viceregal gardens, fifty feet from the spot where I had left the shuttle on half-phase.

The shadowy trees and bushes looked different somehow; wild flowers of a kind I'd never seen before sprouted in the tended beds. Somewhere a nightingale was singing his heart out, ignoring the gunfire.

I was still wearing the ring Bayard had given me, the one with the miniaturized shuttle recall signaler set inside the synthetic ruby. I had left the shuttle in another world-line, with Imperial suppressor beams holding it pinned down like a butterfly on a board, but this wasn't the time to pause and consider things like that. If the signaler worked, I was on the board for another round; if not, the game was finished now. I pressed the stone.

The bird sang. A breeze stirred the long grass. At the far side of the garden, a man stepped into view, capless, dressed in sweat-stained blues. He stopped when he saw me, shouted, and started for me at a run. He was halfway there when the shuttle shimmered and phased into solidity with a rush of displaced air. I stepped inside and flipped the half-phase switch. On the screens, the twilit garden faded to eerie blue. The man who had been running skidded to a stop, raised his gun and fired a full clip into the spot the shuttle occupied. The gun made a remote, flat sound. Then the man threw the gun down and laughed a wild laugh. He turned and wandered away. I could sympathize with him. I knew how he felt. The world had come apart around his ears, and there was no place to turn.

The telltale light on the panel was blinking on, off, on. It was the tracer that had been locked to Roosevelt's shuttle. It still was—and the target was moving.

Again, I didn't stop to calculate the odds. I threw in the drive lever and set off in pursuit.

10

I had seen it before, but it was a thing that could never lose its fascination. All around me, as the hours passed, the world changed and flowed. I knew now that what I was seeing was a simultaneous sequence of A-lines, each differing only slightly from the next, like the frames of a movie film. Nothing really moved; no normal time elapsed during a transdimensional crossing. But the eerie pseudo-activity of E-entropy went on; plants jostled each other for favorable positions; vines attacked trees; weeds swelled and crowded out other weeds. The ivy-covered walls of the palace shrank, broadened, became a fortress ringed with a moat. The walks shifted position, slid away, became footpaths. The trees moved back, gliding slowly through the turf that parted like water, until the shuttle was perched in an open field edged by an ancient forest. The fort had become a stone manor house, with mansard roofs and chimneys poking up into the unchanging sky; the chimneys drew together and merged, became towers of brick with castellated tops.

Suddenly, the hum of the drive whined down-scale and ceased. The scene stabilized. I was looking across a tilled field of grain toward the lone house occupying the top of a low rise among tall trees.

A high stone house with brick towers. Bricks would be red in normal light. Out of all the possible destinations in all the Universes, Roosevelt had led me to the house of Henry Planget.

11

I waited until full dark before I switched the shuttle back to full-phase and stepped out, then shifted it back. The soft *boom*! of imploding air had a lonely sound of finality.

For the past hour, a steady stream of men had come and

gone around the big house. Couriers had galloped up on horseback, and others had ridden away down the unpaved road with full saddlebags slapping at their mounts' flanks. Lights burned in all the ground-floor windows. Sentries paced in front of the main door. Everything about the place spelled military headquarters. Somewhere inside, Roosevelt would be cooking up the last ingredients of his grand scheme for the world.

I skirted the house, came up in the shelter of a row of poplars until I could see through the nearest set of casement windows. A group of men in ornate green uniforms clustered around a table on which a map was spread, under a gas-burning chandelier. Roosevelt wasn't among them. It was the same in the next room, except that the men wore plain khaki and were working over what might have been manning documents or supply lists. I worked my way halfway around the house, using the hedges for concealment, before I found my man. He was sitting alone at a table, writing rapidly with a ball-point pen—a curious anomaly in the old-fashioned setting. He was smiling a little as he wrote. There was a small cut on his forehead. He was still wearing the fancy outfit he had donned for the ceremony back in New Normandy, now stained and powder-burned. It seemed the general had seen some close action before he had left the scene of battle.

He finished writing and left the room. I closed in and checked the windows. It was a mild evening, and they stood open half an inch. Ten seconds later, I was inside.

12

I listened at the door, heard nothing, opened it, and took a look along a papered hallway glowing softly in the light of a single gas jet. A sentry stood at the far end, all shiny leather and brass, with a musket over his shoulder. I tried to pretend I was a shadow moving along the hall, sliding into the recess of a stairwell. He never turned his head.

There was red carpeting on the stairs, a polished mahogany rail. On the landing, I gave a listen, then went on up into a dark corridor, door lined. I was standing there, waiting for instinct to whisper instructions in my ear, when I felt a touch at the hip. I came around fast, and my hand went to the sword-hilt before I understood. The touch had been the sword, tugging gently at my side. I drew it, following the direction of the pull.

13

At the end of the corridor, three steps led up to double doors of carved oak. I pushed through them, stood in moonlight shining through a rose window. It wasn't a room that I had ever seen before—and yet it was. I knew, without knowing how I knew, that it was the analog of the chapel from which Roosevelt had stolen the reliquary box. This room was smaller, simpler, almost unadorned. But somehow, in the abstruse geography of the Net of alternate reality, it occupied the same position. The altar under the high window consisted of two heavy oak uprights with a flat slab of rough stone across them, but somehow, it was the same altar. In the dim light, it looked like an ancient sacrificial block. I started forward and the door made a soft sound behind me. I turned, and Roosevelt stood there. His black eyes seemed to blaze across the darkness at me, as armed men spread out behind him.

"You see, Plantagenet?" he said softly. "Struggle as you will, your fate must deliver you into my hands!"

14

"I misjudged you when we met," Roosevelt said. "And again, in New Normandy. You should have seized on the chance to escape, filled with the zeal to set a nation free. The countryside would have risen at your call; you'd have ridden into glory with your followers at your back and the bright sun overhead. Why didn't you?"

"You're a clever man, Roosevelt," I said. "But not clever enough to play God. Men aren't cardboard cutouts for you to arrange to suit yourself."

"Men are tools," Roosevelt said flatly. "As for you—you're a tool that turns in the hand, and your edges are surpassingly sharp." He shook his head. "You're supposed to be a man of emotion and action, Plantagenet, not thought!"

"Stop second-guessing me, Roosevelt. Your scheme's blown up in your face. You've failed—the way your father failed with Henry Planget." It was a shot in the dark, just something to say. For a moment, he looked startled. Then his teeth flashed in a smile.

"It was my grandfather," he said. "I wonder how you learned of that? But it doesn't matter now, does it? You've come here, to the one place you had to come to—and found me waiting and ready."

"Not so ready. I could have shot you while you were writing at your desk."

"I fail to see the weapon." He was still smiling an almost gentle smile. "No, Plantagenet, it's not your destiny to shoot me in the back. We'll have our meeting face to face—and the fateful time is now." He drew the heavy longsword slung at his side. The light winked on the jewels that crusted the pommel and grip and *pas-d'âne*. The men behind him stood silent, drawn guns in their hands.

"You like to talk about fate, Roosevelt," I said. "It's a lot of hot air. A man determines his own fate." I was watching the long blade, ready to ward off a blow with the broken weapon in my hand. Roosevelt looked at it and laughed, a low chuckle.

"Like your blade, Plantagenet, you're incomplete! You know a little—though even that little surprises me—but not enough. Don't you recognize the weapon you face?"

"It's a fancy piece of iron," I said. "But a weapon is as good as the man behind it."

"Look on Balingore!" Roosevelt held the sword out so that the blade caught the light. It was a slab of edged and polished steel, six feet long, as wide as my hand, and Roosevelt's brawny arm held it as though it were a stick of wood. "It was forged for your once-great ancestor, Richard of the lion-heart. It served him well—but he was a greedy man. He went too far, grew fat on gold and wine. Richard Bombast, they called him in the end. He lay drunk in his chamber while the French attacked the walls of London and his people opened the gates to them. He bought his life with this. He handed it, hilt-first, to the Dutch mercenary who led the forces of Louis Augustus, and swore the submission of himself and his house, to the end of time!"

"Fairy tales," I said.

"But a fairy tale you believe in." Roosevelt tilted the sword, made light wink in my eyes. "I know why you're here, Plantagenet."

"Do you?"

He nodded somberly. "Somehow—and later you'll tell me how—you learned that Balingore was the key object through which the lines of power run. You imagined you could steal it, and win back all that you lost, so long ago." He shook his head. "But the weapon is mine, now! Its touch would shrivel your hand. All the probability energies built up in seven hundred years of history flow through this steel, and every erg of that titanic charge denies your claim. I offer you your last chance for life and its riches, Plantagenet! Submit to me now, and you'll stand first below the throne in the new order. Refuse, and you'll die in an agony beyond your comprehension!"

"Dead is dead," I said. "The method doesn't matter much. Why don't you go ahead, do it now? You've got the weapon in your hand."

"I should have killed you," he said between his teeth. "I should have killed you long ago!"

"You kept me alive for a reason," I said raggedly. "But it wasn't your reason, Roosevelt. All along, you've thought you were in charge, but you weren't. Maybe fate isn't as easy to twist as you thought it was—"

One of the men behind Roosevelt gave a muffled yell; a rat as big as a tomcat scuttled out between his feet. Roosevelt cut at it with the sword—and I whirled and sprinted for the altar.

15

I expected gunfire to racket, a bullet in the spine, a wash of agony from a nerve-gun; but Roosevelt shouted an order to his men to hold their fire. I jumped up on the low platform, gripped the altar-stone, and heaved at it. I might as well have tried to lift the columns of the Parthenon. Roosevelt was coming toward me at a run. I jammed the broken sword in under the rock, felt it clash on metal—

The Universe turned to white fire that fountained round me, then dwindled away to misty gray . . .

16

"My lord, will you attack?" Trumpington's voice came from beside. I looked up at the sun, burning through the mist. I thought of England's green fields, and the sunny vineyards of Aquitaine, of the empire I might yet win. I looked across toward the place where the enemy waited, where I knew death waited with a message for me.

"I will attack," I said.

"My lord," Trumpington's voice was troubled. "Is all well with you?"

"As well as can be with mortal man," I said, and spurred forward toward the high gray walls of Chaluz.

17

The chapel of St. Richard swam back into solidity. Roosevelt was running toward me; behind him, his men were spreading out; one brought his gun up and there was a vivid flash and I felt a smashing blow in my shoulder that spun me back and down....

Roosevelt was standing over me, the bared sword in his hand.

"You can't die yet, Plantagenet," he said in a voice that seemed to ring and echo like a trumpet. "Get on your feet!"

I found my hands and knees, dragged them under me. My body was one pulsating agony ... like the other time, when Renata had shot me with the nerve-gun. Remembering Renata helped. I stood.

"You're a strong man and a proud one," Roosevelt said; his voice swelled and faded. My hand burned and tingled. I remembered the sword, blinked the haze away, saw it still projecting from under the altar-stone where I had jammed it just before somebody shot me. I wished I could get my hands on it.

"You've run a long way, Plantagenet," Roosevelt was saying. "I think you knew how it would end, but still you fought. I admire you for that—and soon I'll let you rest. But first—make your submission to me!"

"You're still afraid..." I got the words out. "You can't swing it ... on your own."

"Listen to me," Roosevelt said. "The storm is all around us; it will reach us here, soon. You've seen it, seen what the Blight is! Unless we resolve the probability flaw now, it will engulf this world-line along with all the rest! You're holding the fault-line open with your stubbornness! In the name of the future of humanity, give up your false pride!"

"There's another solution," I said. "You can submit to me."

"Not though the pit should open to swallow me alive," Roosevelt said, and brought the sword up, poised—

I used the last ounce of strength in my legs to lunge for his wrist, caught it, held him. I reached past him, toward the scarred hilt of my weapon. His hand closed on my wrist. We stood there, locked together, his black eyes inches from mine.

"Stand back!" Roosevelt shouted as his men came close. "I'll break him with my own hands!"

My fingers were six inches from the hilt of the sword. I could feel a current, not a physical pull, but a force as intangible as hate or love flowing from my hand to it.

"Strive, Plantagenet," Roosevelt hissed in my ear, and threw his weight against me. My hand was forced back, away from the sword ...

"Balingore!" I shouted.

The sword moved, leaped across the intervening space to my hand.

18

There was a sensation as though fire poured through my arm, not burning, but scouring away the fatigue. I threw Roosevelt back, and swung six feet of scarred and rusted steel in my two hands. He backed away, his eyes fixed on the old sword, nicked and blunted, but complete now. An expression passed across his face like a man who's looked into the furnace doors of Hell. Then his eyes met mine.

"Again, I underestimated you," he said. "Now I begin to understand who you really are, Plantagenet, *what* you are. But it's far too late to turn back. We meet as we were doomed to meet, face to face, your destiny against mine!" He lunged, and the False Balingore leaped toward me, and the True Balingore flashed out to meet it. The two blades came together with a ring like a struck anvil and the sound filled the world ...

19

... I saw the shaft leap toward me out of the dust, felt the hammer blow in my shoulder that almost struck me from the saddle.

"Sire—you're hit!" Trumpington shouted, and reined closer to me in the press of battle. For an instant weakness swept over me, but I kept my seat, spurred forward.

"My lord—you must retire and let me tend your wound!" Trumpington's voice followed me; but I did not heed him. He galloped abreast, seeking to interpose himself between me and the enemy.

"Sire—turn back!" he shouted. "Even a king can die!"

For a moment we faced each other among the plunging mounts and struggling men.

"More than other men, a king knows how to die," I said. "And when, as well." Then the charge of the enemy host separated us, and I saw him no more. . . .

20

I saw the change come into Roosevelt's eyes, locked on mine as we strained together, chest to chest. He staggered back, staring unbelievingly at his empty hands. Under my eyes, his face withered, his cheeks collapsed, his silks and brocades turned to gray rags that dropped away to expose gaunt ribs, the yellow skin of age. He fell, and his toothless mouth mumbled words, and his hands, like the claws of a bird, scrabbled for a moment at the stone floor. Then there were only bones that dwindled to dust.

The sword burned in my hands. I looked at it and saw how the light shone along the flawless length of the perfect blade, how the jeweled hilt glittered. I sheathed it and walked down the length of the empty chapel and out into the sunlight.

Chapter Eleven

Colonel Bayard was waiting for me in the Imperial Shuttle Garages when I rode the homing beam back. I spent a week in a nice bed under the care of as pretty a nurse as ever raised a temperature. Bayard spent a lot of time with me, filling in the details.

"We've pieced together most of the story," he told me. "Seventy years ago, when the Blight wiped out most of our quantum of alternate world-lines, one man escaped from the general destruction. He was a high official in the government of the key world-line of the Blighted area. He'd been instrumental in the misguided shuttle experimentation that led to the disaster. He managed to coax a crude experimental machine across the Net to the Zero-zero line—one of the very few with a stable enough probability framework to survive the disaster.

"It wasn't a world to his liking. At home, he'd been a power behind the throne of Orange that ruled half the planet. Here he was a nobody—though not without ability. In time, he rose to a top position in the Imperial Trans-Net Liaison Service. But his heart was never in his work. His real ambition was to reestablish the old empire. In his lifetime, he didn't succeed, but he passed the charge on to his son and to his grandson after that.

"Obviously, it was impossible for one man to overthrow the Imperial government single-handed. The van Roosevelts needed another line, outside the Blight, in which to carry out their plan. They picked New Normandy. It was at an adequate technical level, was politically unstable and ripe for a strong hand—and it had a suitable historical base on which to build. Roosevelt's intention was to foment rebellion, play the French against the Britons, and when both sides were exhausted and discredited, step in with a small but highly organized band of irregulars and take over.

"He soon learned the undertaking wasn't as easy as he had supposed. The Duke of Londres was a powerful key figure, not easy to manipulate. He killed him—and discovered that by his interference from outside the line, he'd created a massive probability imbalance with the results you saw here, and at home. He had to restore stability. That meant stamping out the power of the Plantagenets, once and for all, because as long as one of them was alive, anywhere, the probability forces would concentrate in him, force him into the theater of events, and create a probability subnucleus around him. Roosevelt couldn't have that: he needed all the probability energy he could command to make his chosen line stable enough to stand against the Blight.

"Just killing off the Plantagenets wouldn't do. He needed their strength, their *mana,* added to his. That was where you came in. He used some very special instruments that his grandfather had brought with him in his original shuttle from the Orange line to trace the affinities across the Net—and found you. I know you're just a fisherman, you know nothing about the Plantagenets. But the probability lines were concentrated around you. He intended to use you as a figurehead to restore the stability of the New Normandy line, let you destroy your power in a hopeless war, then offer you escape. The price would be your acknowledgment of him as master.

"He made his first mistake when he secretly arrested the Chief of Intelligence, Baron von Richthofen. Manfred has friends; we weren't content with Roosevelt's story of a sudden stroke. Either he was too soft-hearted, or he was afraid to break too many important life-lines in the Imperium. He should have killed him, and me, too. But he didn't.

"They broke me out of the cell I was in a few hours after he left with you on his mission into the Blight. We tried to follow, but the storm blew up, and we barely made it back. When Roosevelt didn't return, we started searching. Our instruments pinpointed him in New Normandy. When I arrived, it was all over—as you know. We haven't found a trace of Roosevelt. I suppose he was killed in the fighting. You're lucky to be alive yourself."

There were a few holes in Bayard's version of what had happened, but that was all right. It covered the main points; it seemed to satisfy everybody. With Roosevelt's death, the storm had blown itself out. There were no more toadstools sprouting in the archives. And Imperial umpires were rapidly pacifying New Normandy under a free parliament.

But there was still something bothering Bayard. When I left the hospital, he showed me the city, took me to restaurants and concerts, fixed me up with a nice little apartment for as long as I wanted it. He didn't mention taking me back home, and neither did I. It was as though we were both waiting for something impending hanging over everything.

We were sitting at a table at a terrace restaurant in Uppsala when I asked him about it. At first he tried to pass it off lightly, but I caught his eyes and held them.

"You'll have to tell me sooner or later," I said. "It concerns me, doesn't it?"

He nodded. "There's still an imbalance in the Net. It's unimportant now, but in time it will grow until it threatens the stability of the Imperium—and of B-I Three, and New Normandy; of every viable line in the quantum. The Blight is a cancer that can never be contained permanently. There's an incompleteness there, and like an electric circuit, it must complete itself."

"Go on."

"Our instruments indicate that the aborted lines center on you, and in the sword Balingore."

I nodded. "I'm not a part of this line, is that it? You'll have to take me back to Key West, then, and let me get on with my fishing."

"It's not as simple as that. Seven hundred years ago a key figure in the ancestral line entered into a course of action that ended by creating the holocaust. Stability will never be attained until the probability lines that were scattered then are led back to their source."

That was all he said, but I understood what he was trying to tell me.

"Then I have to go back," I said. "Into the Blight."

"It's your decision," he said. "The Imperium won't try to force you."

I stood up. The sunset colors had never looked lovelier, the distant music more appealing.

"Let's go," I said.

2

The technicians who checked us into the shuttle worked silently and efficiently. They shook hands all around and we strapped in, Bayard and I.

"Our target is the former master-line of the quantum," Bayard said. I didn't tell him I'd been there before. The shapes and colors of the Blight flowed around us, but for once I didn't notice.

"What will happen afterward?" I asked.

"Our hope is when the Blight energies are canceled, the Blight itself will dissipate instantly. The ruined worlds will no longer exist in the Net."

We didn't talk any more after that. It seemed like only minutes before we clocked down and the hum of the drive died.

"We've arrived," Bayard said. He cycled the lock open and I looked out into shifting fog. It shifted and blew away and the jungle and the ruins were gone, and gleaming towers rose up into sunlight, above green lawns and the play of light in fountains. Far away, a woman was singing.

"I wish there was something I could say," Bayard said. "But there isn't. Good-bye, Mr. Curlon."

I stepped down onto the ground, and the door closed behind me. I waited until the shuttle had vanished in a shimmer of light. Then I walked forward along a flower-bordered path toward the sound of Ironel's voice.

EPILOGUE

Baron von Richthofen, Chief of Imperial Intelligence, looked at Bayard across the polished expanse of desk.

"Your mission was successful, Brion," he said quietly. "At the instant the subject entered the Blighted line, the stress indicators dropped to zero readings across the board. The peril to the Net is ended."

"I wonder," Bayard said, "what he felt, in those last seconds?"

"Nothing. Nothing at all. In one silent instant of readjustment, the continuum closed in to seal the scar. The probability equation is satisfied." Richthofen paused a moment. "Why? Did you see something there?"

"Nothing," Bayard said. "Just fog, as dense as concrete, silent as death."

"He was a brave man, Brion. He fulfilled his destiny."

Bayard nodded, frowning.

"Brion, is there something else—something that troubles you?"

"We've always held the theory that history is immutable," Bayard said. "Perhaps I'm just deluding myself. But I seem to remember a story of King Richard's massacre of the barons at Runnymede. I checked the references to make sure, and I was wrong, of course."

Richthofen looked thoughtful. "The idea has a certain feel of familiarity . . . but that's illusory, of course," he added. "It was King John who met with the barons—and signed their Magna Charta."

"Where did I get the idea that John was executed by Richard in 1201?"

Richthofen started to nod, then checked himself. "For a moment—but no, I recall now. Richard was no longer living then. He was killed by a cross-bow bolt in a minor skirmish at a place called Chaluz, in 1199." He looked thoughtful. "Curious . . . there was no need for him to have taken part in the engagement at all—and after he was wounded, he refused all medical aid. It was almost as though he sought death in battle."

"It was all so clear," Bayard said. "How he lived to a ripe old age—an overripe old age—lost his crown, died in disgrace. I'd swear I read it as a kid. But none of that's in the books. It never happened."

"No," Richthofen said. "It never happened. If it had, the worlds we know would never have existed."

"Still—it's strange."

"Every phenomenon in the space-time probability continuum is strange, Brion—one no more than another."

"I suppose it was just a dream," Bayard said. "A vivid dream."

"Life itself is a dream, they say." Richthofen sat up, suddenly brisk. "But this is the dream we're in, Brion. And we have work waiting for us."

Bayard returned his smile.

"You're right," he said. "One dream is enough for any man."